To
Constance and Anthony Rye

EX LIBRIS

VINTAGE CLASSICS

CONFERENCE AT
COLD COMFORT FARM

Stella Gibbons was born in London in 1902. She went to the North London Collegiate School and studied journalism at University College, London. She worked for various newspapers including the *Evening Standard*. Stella Gibbons is the author of twenty-five novels, three volumes of short stories, and four volumes of poetry. Her first publication was a book of poems, *The Mountain Beast* (1930), and her first novel, *Cold Comfort Farm* (1932), won the Femina Vie Heureuse Prize for 1933. Amongst her works are *Christmas at Cold Comfort Farm* (1940), *Westwood* (1946), *Conference at Cold Comfort Farm* (1949) and *Starlight* (1967). She was elected a Fellow of the Royal Society of Literature in 1950. In 1933 she married the actor and singer Allan Webb. They had one daughter.

Stella Gibbons died in 1989.

ALSO BY STELLA GIBBONS

STELLA GIBBONS

Conference at Cold Comfort Farm

WITH AN INTRODUCTION BY
Libby Purves

VINTAGE BOOKS
London

Published by Vintage 2011

2 4 6 8 10 9 7 5 3

First published in Great Britain by Longmans, Green and Co Ltd

Vintage
Random House, 20 Vauxhall Bridge Road,
London SW1V 2SA

www.vintage-classics.info

Addresses for companies within The Random House Group Limited
can be found at: www.randomhouse.co.uk/offices.htm

The Random House Group Limited Reg. No. 954009

A CIP catalogue record for this book
is available from the British Library

ISBN 9780099528685

The Random House Group Limited supports The Forest Stewardship
Council (FSC®), the leading international forest certification organisation.
Our books carrying the FSC label are printed on FSC® certified paper. FSC
is the only forest certification scheme endorsed by the leading environmental
organisations, including Greenpeace. Our paper procurement policy can be
found at www.randomhouse.co.uk/environment

MIX
Paper from
responsible sources
FSC
www.fsc.org
FSC® C016897

Typeset in Bembo by Palimpsest Book Production Limited,
Falkirk, Stirlingshire

Printed and bound by CPI Group (UK) Ltd, Croydon, CR0 4YY

Introduction

This contains elements of the plot

When I talked with Stella Gibbons in her old age – a dryly amusing, friendly presence in her Highgate eyrie – she ruefully admitted that she missed the imaginative world of *Cold Comfort Farm*, and had never quite matched its spirit in her later writings. That timeless spoof of heaving emotionality grew partly from high-spirited mockery of Thomas Hardy, Hugh Walpole and Mary Webb, and partly from a heartfelt reaction against her own temperamental father and turbulent family life. So the first novel sprang up as first novels should: natural as tangleweed, sharp as sukebind, a larky testament from a young woman making her way in 1930's London. Working for the *Evening Standard*, longing for love and progress and another kind of life, she would read out its jokes to amuse her work-mates and cheer herself up in the Lyons' Corner House after hours.

Seventeen years later, on the far side of wartime austerity and with sixteen books published, Gibbons could not resist allowing her imagination to revisit the farm and contemplate its changes related to the current state of the world. In *Conference at Cold Comfort Farm* we are in the age of compulsory tidying, planned societies, Utopian dreams and bossy officialdom: a time when untidy, run-down historic buildings were being taken over by the National Trust and filled with 'rustick' dressers and arty pottery and weekend visitors. In *Cold Comfort Farm* Mrs Smiling devoted herself to collecting brassieres and the search for the perfect one but here she engages with the era of managerial revolution, of arrogant science and political functionaries like Mrs Ernestine Thump in her 'piteously unsuccessful hat', a piggy-eyed bossy-boots, 'from whose photograph Flora had often averted her eyes in the daily journals.'

And of course, this change presents a conundrum for the author and her avatar Flora: for in *Cold Comfort Farm* Flora was the *sole* representative of organization, planning, rationality and calm. So Flora must find new adversaries. And she does: the intellectual Mybug, an incidental running joke in the first book, becomes central in *Conference at Cold Comfort Farm*. His world of cutting-edge art and New Thought, what Flora thinks of as 'the second Dark Ages', is the enemy now. He has moved on, no longer embracing Lawrentian ideas of 'deep, dark, bitter belly-tension' between man and woman, but inclining towards the doctrines of psychoanalysis and progressive education. In a nice swipe at A.S.Neill's educational theory, Mybug's children go to 'Badlands' and have only fifteen minutes of child-chosen total recall from a chosen teacher everyday, then 'just fool around'. Mybug has surrounded himself with European artists of the new vogue, modernists who far from suppressing nasty memories of the woodshed, have brought every nasty thing out into the open to celebrate it. Mybug reveres their doctrines and works with all the blind stubborn determination which was once deployed by the rustics in their belief that there must 'always be Starkadders at Cold Comfort Farm.'

This time, Flora and Reuben are on the same side from the start: positively nostalgic for the old disorderly Starkadder ways, muck and magic, sukebind and water-voles and taking the bull to the cow. Who would not be, when the alternative is having old buildings suffering under labels like 'Ye Olde Pantrie' and 'The Lytel Store Roome' and being hired out for conferences rather than being lived, and ranted, in by their traditional occupants?

The poor old farm, 'all cockered up like a lost woman on Worthing front', has lost its last Starkadder to the agricultural efficiency revolution and Mr Parker-Poke from the Ministry (the author never lost her gift for perfect names). It must be saved. Given back, even, to the old Starkadder ways. And in the quest for enemies to save it from, Gibbons happily lighted on new targets. Fascinatingly, these adversaries are more familiar to us in the twenty-first century than her dark-blooded emotional rustics were to her mid-twentieth century readers.

The Conference attracts a slew of post-war intellectuals and artists, ripe for guying. Here – loosely disguised – are Picasso, Moore, Britten, Kafka, Anouilh and Sartre: here are fashionable swamis and sullen poets, a seductive female existentialist called Mdlle Avaler and Greetë Grümbl from Sweden lecturing on 'Angst, its causes and cultivation.' The cruel plot-summary of Bob Flatte's new opera *The Flayed* is perhaps harsher than *Peter Grimes* deserves – if indeed that was the opus on her mind, which seems suspiciously likely. Britten's dark opera was first played four years earlier.

And *The Dromedary* is certainly unfairly unkind to Kafka, with the same reservation.

On first reading the book in my teens I was a little indignant at her breezy philistinism, but now I think differently. We may hugely admire some of those she sends up: but all the same, there is a bracing quality in her contempt, just as there was in her ridiculing of trauma and heaving emotion in *Cold Comfort Farm*. Emotion is real and important, so is artistic innovation: but both are susceptible to wallowing, exaggeration, posing and exploitation by the vain and selfish. That is the quality which Gibbons sends up so mercilessly, and it is good for any age to tilt at the slavish admiration of the Mybugs. When he admires a verbal spat at the picnic, crooning that the conversation was 'coruscatingly malicious . . . slow, heavy, brutally impenetrable', it is not hard to find modern parallels in certain salons of mutual admiration which are still among us. One finds oneself thinking of Martin Amis and his circle. Or BBC Two's Newnight Review. While some of Gibbons's targets have dated – the scientists are oddly unrecognisable, though some of them were no doubt the Huxleys – others have not. Overrated artists are still walking alongside their better peers; Hacke, Messe, and Claude Hubris survive in the age of the Young British Artists, the Saatchi Gallery, Tate Modern and performance art. And we are free to raise an eyebrow and play the Philistine if we feel like it: at times, in grimmer exhibitions, the Starkadder women say it for all of us when they weep their eyes out over the artworks in the 'Greate Barne', flinging skirts over their heads and crying 'Tes th' poor souls as made 'em as we be weepin' for . . . fancy wantin' to make such things, Miss Poste! Poor souls, poor souls.' There will always be art fit to 'turn t'milk mooky' and we must always be free to say so.

Time winnows out much, and polishes understanding of the rest: some of the works Gibbons mocks have become iconic, understood and revered for the best of reasons. Yet mockery has its uses as much as earnest criticism. Every artistic movement needs is philistines, though it may not be grateful to them at the time.

The pleasure of *Conference at Cold Comfort Farm* is a different tenor to the charms of its predecessor. And curiously, for those who loved the murderous murk of *Cold Comfort Farm* before Flora reformed it, there is consolation in the final happy scenes of this book. The Starkadders, crazy primitives, are throwing out the self-tortured preening culturati. Our Micah is a-cursing, Our Mark and Our Luke are fist-fighting, and Our Caraway is throwing National Trust furniture out of the window after chasing some random brother across the 'Great Yarde' with a chopper. 'I likes fine to see 'em all a-bashing and a-cursin' cries Charley, and secretly, so do we. The catch-up is worth having. It is reassuring to know that Elfine's poetry is no better, that Seth the movie star is going bald, and that old Adam Lambsbreath is finally reunited with his beloved dish-mop.

Libby Purves, 2011

I think it necessary to make a stand against
the encroachments of black bile.

Thomas Love Peacock.

1

On a sunny morning in the midst of the Second Dark Ages, Flora and Charles Fairford were seated at breakfast with their family in the vicarage overlooking the Regent's Park in London where they had lived since Charles's ordination some thirteen years ago. Flora, it may be remembered, had been Flora Poste noted for the straightness of her nose and the efficacy of her restorative work at Cold Comfort Farm in Sussex. The nose retained its classic elegance; the work she seldom thought of nowadays, for Flora had five children. The post had just arrived, and the family party was occupied in reading its letters.

Flora's were typical of those usually received by the wife of a vicar in a large poor parish, but among the appeals and reports was an envelope, lined with scarlet and addressed in a tortured yet dashing hand, which caused her, when she had glanced at the letter's signature, to exclaim in surprise. No one took any notice. Her husband was busy with his own correspondence, and the children were busy eating.

'I say, listen to this,' commanded Flora, and began to read aloud:

'My Dear Flora Fairford,

Of course you won't remember me. You've probably forgotten my name. I hesitated about contacting you. But last night I saw your married name in the book while looking up Messe the Transitorist craftsman, and . . . the Idea came. I'll be frank with you. The I.T.G. is holding a conference at Cold Comfort Farm (remember, Flora?) from June 17th to the 24th, and I'm acting as Organizing Secy. Can you come down and help? You could organize . . . once.'

'What's the I.T.G.?' interrupted Flora's eldest daughter.

'International Thinkers' Group,' said the eldest son, without glancing up from a book propped on his knees below the table.

'*Does that put you on your mettle?*' the letter went on. ('I haven't got a mettle,' muttered Flora. 'Alex, put that Latin grammar away and finish your breakfast.') And then she added impressively:

'Who do you think it's from? Mr Mybug!'

Her family looked blank, with the exception of Charles, who frowned.

'Oh no, of course. None of you were born,' Flora went on. 'You remember, don't you, my love?' to Charles.

'Vaguely. But you can't go, Flora; it's the American Tea and Bazaar on the 17th.'

'So it is. I forgot. No, I can't; it's out of the question,' and Flora put the letter away in her skirt pocket and said no more.

But after breakfast, when the elder children had gone to school, and Emilia the baby was watching the spiv (allotted to Flora to help her with household duties because she was the mother of five) holystoning the kitchen floor, Flora went to the telephone and dialled a number.

After a pause, excessive even for the Second Dark Ages, a voice said faintly:

'Hullo? Yes, I should say?'

'Is that you, Sneller? Is Mrs Smiling at home?'

'If you will hold the line, madam, I will ascertain. What name shall I say, madam?'

'It's me, Mrs Fairford, Sneller.'

'Very good, madam.'

There was the sound of footsteps creeping away, and after another excessive pause another voice, low and with a bewitching American lilt, said:

'Hullo there?'

'Mary? It's me. I say, can I come to tea this afternoon?'

'Lovely, but I must just ask Sneller.'

'Mary, do you *still* have to get permission from your butler every time you want to ask anyone to the house? I do think that after all these years –'

'It isn't that; it upsets him if he has to see about cakes and everything. Hold on.'

There was one more excessive pause, and then Mrs Smiling came back and said that it was all right and she would love to see Flora about four o'clock.

So just after four o'clock that afternoon Flora rang the bell of 1, Mouse Place. It had not suffered in Recent Events, but it had been shut up with Sneller as caretaker while Mrs Smiling was in the United States, and Flora had not seen it for many years. However, Mrs Smiling had

3

friends in high and low places, and she had contrived to get the house painted. It looked fresh and elegant in the summer sunlight, and there were Sweet Williams in the metal baskets hanging from its balcony.

Sneller, Mrs Smiling's butler, opened the door. He was now so old as to cause no emotion in the beholder beyond incredulity at his being yet with us, and he was still exactly like a tortoise.

'Good afternoon, Sneller. How nice to see you again after this long time.'

'And to see you, madam. I hope you are keeping well, madam, and Mr Fairford, and all the young ladies and gentlemen.'

Flora replied that they were well, and, reflecting that Sneller's *all* made her family sound even larger than it was, followed him across the hall, her grey skirts whispering along the mosaic floor of flowers and shells.

Mrs Smiling came out of the drawing-room to greet her. Time had been gentle with Mrs Smiling's grey eyes and beautiful mouth, and she wore a dove-coloured dress almost to her ankles and a crystal necklace. But, to Flora's dismay, she saw a Bulk seated upon the drawing-room sofa beyond her friend's shoulder: a female Bulk with a lot of hair and little glistening eyes under a piteously unsuccessful hat.

'Who's that?' she breathed, stooping to kiss her friend lightly.

'Mrs Ernestine Thump. S'sh, Flora! I can't help it,' breathed back Mrs Smiling, and led the way into the drawing-room.

Mrs Ernestine Thump was sitting very squarely on the

sofa, surrounded by red, white and blue papers. The hat had too plainly been clapped on to her pate at an expensive shop in a dutiful attempt to look smart, and Flora now recognized her as a female holding on to a public position, from whose photograph she had often averted her eyes in the daily journals.

'Ernestine, this is Flawra. Flawra, you don't know Ernestine,' said Mrs Smiling, and her American accent became more noticeable, as it always did when she was slightly agitated. 'I met Ernestine on the *Queen* the last time I came over; she was coming back from going over to see about what they think about nutritional equivalents over there,' she ended vaguely.

Flora saw that Ernestine Thump was opening her mouth to ask her what she Did? So she quickly smiled and bowed to her and dashed without pause into an account of Mr Mybug's letter and the Conference of the International Thinkers' Group.

'You are supposed to be opening the Bazaar for us on the 17th, Mary, but I am anxious to accept Mr Mybug's invitation, and I was going to suggest –'

'Of course! Don't miss it for anything! Glorious opportunity! How I wish I could be with you! Internationally famous names! Feast of culture!' shouted Mrs Ernestine Thump. 'Of course We believe in artists, and thinkers! They're no use practically, but it looks well to have them! Provided they will co-operate in raising the general level of culture and if their tone is democratically sound We have nothing against them! Who's going to be there? Ah, thank you,' as Flora silently handed her a leaflet about the Conference enclosed by

Mr Mybug in his letter. At the same moment Sneller crept in with the tea.

In a moment Mrs Ernestine Thump began reading names aloud from the leaflet.

'Claudie Hubris, eh? Great friend of mine! He's done well, very well! He's Executive Technical Adviser for Nutritional Necessities Inc.; it has branches all over the Globe! They've bought out most of the other Trusts! Treat their people decently, too! Oh, you'll like Claudie! He's a worker and a grand person into the bargain!'

She swallowed a tea-cake and filled her mouth with tea and swished it about.

'Peccavi! Painter Portuguese, isn't he? Do you know his stuff? I went to the Private View of his last show here! Odd stuff, very odd, but it had quite something! Of course he went through Hell in the trouble out there!'

So did the people who went through his last show here, thought Flora.

'Are they having an art show at the Conference?' enquired Mrs Smiling, frowning slightly at Flora, who was looking mutinous.

'Sculpture, painting, readings from unpublished works *and* a one-day Exhibition of Transitorist Art!' Mrs Ernestine Thump waved the leaflet in her face. 'Now who else is there? Thanks,' accepting the last tea-cake. (Flora saw Sneller make a gesture, at once hopeless and threatening, at Mrs Smiling, who looked distressed. She began to fear that Mrs Thump was never going home, for although all the food had gone there was still tea in the pot and sugar and milk in the basin and jug.)

'Messe, Transitorist craftsman,' continued Mrs Ernestine

Thump, gnawing the tea-cake and scattering crumbs as she read. 'Hacke, sculptor. Tom Jones, poet, contributor to the quarterly journal *Nadir*. Mdlle Adrienne Avaler, representing the Existentialist Movement –'

'Oh, yes! Existentialism. Now, do tell me – what *is* Existentialism?' exclaimed Flora and Mrs Smiling together, but before Mrs Thump had time to banish a slightly baffled expression which for the first time clouded her bluff *arriviste* countenance, Mrs Smiling went on in her low, soft, vague voice:

'Isn't it just *being*? What I mean is, I read in some French magazine; my French is not awfully good –'

'We plan to make it compulsory for everybody, everywhere!' bellowed Mrs Ernestine Thump, beginning (to Flora's relief) to gather up her papers.

'– and so far as I could make out, if you are an Existentialist you *go to the facts themselves in all their innocence, interrogating them without asking any leading questions and waiting patiently for their answer.*'

'No time for that!' shouted Mrs Ernestine Thump, heaving herself up from the sofa. 'Can't wait! Get on with the job! Plenty for everybody to do nowadays!' and her glistening little eye was fixed upon Mrs Smiling, who looked as if she had plenty of time and nothing to do in it.

'Another thing it said was,' continued Mrs Smiling, '*Life is not a problem to be solved but a reality to be experienced*. I liked that, myself.'

'All this is Above My Head,' announced Mrs Ernestine Thump – jokingly, of course. 'I leave *you* to deal with the Ideas, ladies, and I must Run Off. I've got a Committee at five, I'm seeing my dentist at six (he makes an exception for me, dear man), and then down to the House. You two girls are jolly lucky,' she added with sinister jocularity as she bustled past Sneller, who was attempting to show her out, and nearly sent him flying, 'if your grading permits you to sit here chin-wagging! *You*' – pointing a finger in a dirty glove at Flora – 'get off on the score of having children under fourteen, I presume, but how about *you*' – transferring the finger to Mrs Smiling. 'Delicate health? Aged parents?'

'Sneller, my butler,' drawled Mrs Smiling. 'While being responsible for my delicate health, he also stands to me *in loco parentis*. Good-bye, Ernestine. Come again soon.'

Through the window they watched Mrs Ernestine Thump shoehorning herself into a small car driven by a depressed-looking girl, and then being driven away.

'My dear Mary, what people you do take up with,' sighed Flora, leaning back in her chair.

'Mrs Ernestine Thump is a very good woman who does a lot of valuable public work,' replied Mrs Smiling reprovingly.

'All right; never mind her now. If the Bazaar on the 17th could be postponed, I could go to the Conference. Could you be ill for a week, Mary?'

'Surely. But, Flora, are you really sure you want to go? I thought some of those people – Peccavi and Hacke and so forth – sounded a bit much.'

'It isn't the Conference really, it's Cold Comfort Farm. I have not had any news from there for over five years. Mary, I *do feel* that all is not well at the farm.'

Mrs Smiling poured herself out a cup of tepid tea and

answered that considering what sort of a place the Farm was, and what kind of people lived there, it would be surprising if all were well. 'Like the human race,' she ended pensively. 'What was the last news you had from the Farm?'

'Reuben used to send me a card every Christmas with "Best regards from Coz. Reuben" on it, and the last one I received also said, *"All th' chaps but me and Urk has gone to South Afriky".*'

'It does not tell one much.'

'No.'

'Was Reuben's writing agitated or barely legible?'

'Not more barely legible than usual. I used to hear regularly from Elfine Hawk-Monitor, but since her husband got his knighthood and went to Washington I have not heard so often, and during Recent Events, of course, some of her letters may have been lost. So I have had no news from her for some time.'

'It seems strange that a Conference should be held at the farm.'

'It *is* strange, Mary; it is very strange indeed, and that is just what disturbs me. Can there no longer be Starkadders at Cold Comfort?'

'Perhaps they have hired it out by the week. You would not put that past them, would you?'

'No, indeed. And yet – I do not know. They all had a fierce passion for the place. I do not think they would hire it out to strangers.'

'And such strangers!' Mrs Smiling picked up the leaflet dropped by Mrs Ernestine Thump. *'Representatives of the Managerial Revolutionary Party will attend the Conference,'* she read aloud. 'What in heck is that?'

'Well, broadly speaking, they are experts. They possess technical knowledge which most ordinary people do not possess. For instance, suppose absolutely everything except a few things were simply blown sky-high and we were all rushing about with nothing to eat and no pure water and no artificial heat and no clothes and no houses and frightful diseases everywhere –'

Flora paused for breath, and Mrs Smiling sipped her tea and said: 'Do go on.'

'And then suppose there were a few people who understand how to build gas-mains and collect electricity or whatever it is you do, they would have a terrific advantage over all the people who knew nothing about it, wouldn't they? They could, and would, *manage* all of us, as well as *managing* the gas-mains. It would be a *managerial* revolution.'

'I suppose so. But I don't like the idea.'

'Nobody does. Everybody is afraid of them. The trouble is, of course, that they are both necessary and *fearfully useful*.'

'I get you. And some of them will be at this Cawnference?'

'Yes.' Flora now read aloud from the leaflet.

'*Delegates from the Managerial Revolutionary Party will include Production Managers, Operating Executives, Superintendents, Administrative Engineers and Supervisory Technicians.*'

'It doesn't say anything about gas-mains, and I don't think you will like being there, Flawra.'

'I know.'

And Flora reflected for a moment. (Sneller was now shakily removing the tea. What he had thought of Mrs Ernestine Thump, Mrs Smiling did not dare to imagine.)

Flora knew that if she went to the Conference she would be buttonholed just when she wanted to be quiet, and asked her opinion of this or that or (worse still) what was going to happen about the other; she would daily be confronted by huge faces bursting with pseudo-energy and thrusting their views down her throat hocus-pocus and willy-nilly; there would also be long, nervous faces timidly intimating that nothing was going to be any use anyway, so why do it? and, worst of all, there would be the Works of Peccavi, Hacke and Messe, to say nothing of themes from Bob Flatte's new opera *The Flayed* blown (as she had just observed when her glance fell on the leaflet) by the composer himself upon a recorder. No, thought Flora, I will write to Mr Mybug and tell him that I cannot go.

'I think it is your duty to go, Flawra,' suddenly said Mrs Smiling.

'I feared you would say that, Mary.' And Flora sighed.

'I am not thinking of all those intellectuals and people. They like it. I am thinking of your Cousin Reuben, who always sounded such a nice guy, and that girl he married, and the farm itself —'

'And the International Thinkers, Mary!' exclaimed Flora, suddenly taking fire. 'All those poor souls! I might be able to help them! I *do feel* —'

'That remark always means that your Florence Nightingale complex is raging, Flawra. And "those poor souls" include the most prarminent exponents of arl that is most vital and dynamic —'

'That will do, Mary; I am not a Women's Club in Negaunee. If you think I ought to go, I will. I think I ought to, too. I will begin to make arrangements at once.'

'Give me time to work up my grippe, darling.'

'I forgot your illness, Mary. But have no fears; I will make the preliminary arrangements in secret.'

'Can you go awf, and leave Charles, and all the children, just like that?' marvelled Mrs Smiling, accompanying her friend through the hall.

'Of course not; it will need Herculean efforts; it always does. But Charles can, at need, be self-supporting, the spiv is devoted to the children, and finally the Vicarage will be guarded by the great boarhound Cripps. Good-bye, dear Mary; except for your awful friend it was a lovely tea.'

Mrs Smiling was taken ill two days before the 17th of June, so Flora was able to telephone to Mr Mybug and tell him that circumstances permitted her to fall in with his suggestion.

'Oh "stout work"!' cried Mr Mybug, with all his former boyish enthusiasm. 'I'm . . . pretty grateful, Flora. You don't mind my using the old name, do you?'

It's all the same if I do, thought Flora.

'And I say – great luck!' continued Mr Mybug. 'Peccavi is lending us his great painting *The Excreta* and *he's bringing Riska!*'

Flora made an interrogative sound.

'You know her, of course. She's been his model for six months now . . . the loveliest thing in de Salazar's Portugal.'

'How delightful!'

'Of course, they're neither of them easy,' warned Mybug. 'Sexual tension between them is very strong.'

That will be fun, thought Flora.

'And Hacke, the sculptor, is lending *Woman with Child* and *Woman with Wind*. They're priceless, of course; no firm will insure them, so Hacke and I are travelling down with them in the guard's van. My dear lady, no *car* is strong enough to take them!' in reply to a suggestion from Flora, 'and I couldn't charter a lorry. They are enormous, of course; monumental; Assyrian.'

That made it more difficult to avoid seeing them. But Flora was not going to turn back now.

'And Messe has promised, as you saw by the advance publicity I sent you, to do us a one-day show of Transitorist Craft work. Do you know his stuff? He won't use materials lasting longer than one day, and he mostly works in pastry made from national flour, contemporary sausage-meat, and modern dyestuffs. Of course, I don't put him within *miles* of Peccavi. I should put him somewhere between Pushe and Dashitoffski.'

'I see that a delegate from the East is expected,' said Flora, thinking of places to put Messe.

'Oh yes, a sort of a sage; I don't know his name. And Tom Jones; he's got a food fixation, but otherwise he's all right. You'll like Tom.'

'How is Rennett?' asked Flora, having heard quite enough about the delegates.

'Oh, Rennett is – Rennett,' returned Mr Mybug, with a light laugh. 'We've got three boys, you know. Healthy enough, but they've all three got fixations on us. I've had them analysed; no good.'

'Dear me, I am sorry. Er – what form does the fixation take?'

'Oh, liking to be with us, wanting to be kissed good

night, and that sort of thing. We've tried everything – it only gets worse.'

'Do they go to school?'

'Heavens, yes; we sent Trafford at eighteen months. They all go to a progressive school – Badlands, at Edgware. No rules, no lessons, no teachers. The children listen to total recall from a member of the staff chosen by themselves for fifteen minutes every morning. Otherwise they just fool about. By the way, have *you* any family?'

Flora answered that she had five, but, not wishing to hear Mr Mybug's comments upon their stodgy schools, she went on hastily:

'Oh, perhaps you can tell me. What has happened to the Farm? Why is a Conference being held there? Aren't there Starkadders at Cold Comfort any more?'

Mr Mybug replied indifferently that he really did not know. He had heard no news of the Farm for years. It was Tom Jones who had suggested it as a meeting-place for the Conference, and he had written to The Occupier asking if the dates were free. The name appeared on a list of premises to be hired for conferences and he, Mr Mybug, presumed that it had been taken over by some trust or committee of sorts; it was just the sort of place that might have been. He knew nothing about the Starkadders nowadays.

'I say, *have* you read *The Dromedary*?' he said suddenly. 'I don't expect you have, but it's *superb*.'

'Yes, I have,' retorted Flora, controlling an impulse to add, *So there, see?*

'And what did you think of it?'

'I thought it marvellous,' replied Flora with truth,

reflecting that the passing years had done nothing to mitigate Mr Mybug's boundless asininity.

Mr Mybug seemed to want to go on talking about *The Dromedary*, but Flora ended their conversation by making a brief and definite arrangement to meet his train outside Beershorn Station at four o'clock on the afternoon of the following Sunday, June 16th, and rang off.

2

She herself travelled down by coach, and all the children, the spiv and the great boarhound Cripps came to the end of the road, where the coach stopped, to see her off.

Charles was unable to be present because he was teaching in Sunday School, but he kissed her a most tender good-bye and told her to enjoy (if it were possible to do so) her visit. He suspected that Mrs Smiling's grippe was all baloney, and Flora knew that he suspected, and he knew that she knew, but neither mentioned it, and so the Parish was peacefully diddled and Flora went off in a placid frame of mind.

'Good-bye, Mamma, good-bye!' the children cried, waving frantically as Flora climbed into the coach, and the baby danced up and down upon the spiv's padded shoulders, which were admirably designed for such exercise. The great boarhound Cripps bayed, the coach moved forward, and her journey had begun.

'Good-bye, dear, dear Mamma! Good-bye!'

'Good-bye! *Don't forget to feed the parrot!*' cried Flora through the window, in the phrase popular in the dear dead frivolous Twenties, and all the children shrieked back, '*What parrot?*' just as they were meant to do. Flora sat down and, after one furtive glance at her fellow passengers to see if one of them looked like Peccavi, she opened *Vogue*, and hardly raised her eyes from it until, some hours later, the coach stopped outside the little station at Beershorn in the midst of the Sussex Downs.

Flora alighted, and the coach went on its way towards the coast. She walked into the station, where the train of course had not arrived although it was twenty minutes overdue, and amused herself by inspecting well-remembered places: the waiting-room and offices suggesting those of an old-fashioned lazar-house, the rennet post to which Viper the gelding had been tethered by the ancient cowman Adam Lambsbreath on the night of her arrival sixteen years ago, the posters of the Owl and the Waverley Pen and Margaret Lockwood and Patricia Roc flapping drearily in the wind.

Presently a car twenty feet long, with a huge, prosperous man sitting in the back and an Oriental at the wheel, drove into the station yard. At the same time an old-fashioned brake, drawn by two horses and driven by a local character, came down the hill and stopped at the other side of the road. Thinking that this must be the conveyance provided for the delegates, Flora left the station and crossed the road towards the brake.

Someone was sitting in it, nursing a paper bag, whose appearance was vaguely familiar to her, and she approached him, affecting not to hear a hissing noise behind her indicating that the Oriental chauffeur had alighted and was trying to attract her attention, probably to ask her the way to the Farm.

She reached the brake, and resting one hand upon its

back wheel and with the other shading her eyes from the sun, gazed up at its solitary occupant. At the same instant he rose to his feet.

'Reuben!' exclaimed Flora.

'Cousin Flora!' said Reuben, as near joyfully as a Starkadder could. 'Why, I'd a know'd ee anywheer, coz, and right glad I am to shake ee again by th' hand, soul!'

They exchanged a hearty handclasp over the side of the brake. The chauffeur was still hissing away in the background, but Flora took no notice.

'I will come down an' join ee, Cousin Flora,' said Reuben, beginning to descend. 'Will ee drive wi' me in th' buggy (I'll lay ee remembers th' buggy?) back to – to th' – th' old place? Th' buggy du be up th' hill, in th' liddle lane.'

'I should like that above everything, Reuben, and you must tell me all your news; how Amos is getting on in America, and about Aunt Ada Doom, and all the other Starkadders – are they still in South Africa? and Nancy – have you any more children? – but first I must go down and meet the ladies and gentlemen who are coming for the Conference. I am helping Mr Mybug (you remember him?) to arrange everything.'

'A fat chap wi' fuzzled hair, allus jawin',' nodded Reuben. 'Ay, I remember un well.'

'Was it you to whom Mr Jones wrote about holding the Conference at the Farm?' Flora went on, as they walked across the yard together.

The Oriental chauffeur followed them, still hissing.

Reuben paled beneath his tan. 'Nay, Cousin Flora,' he answered in a low, choked voice.

Flora glanced at him in surprise, but the train had now

arrived, and there was no time for further conversation. Hastily promising to meet her cousin in the little lane as soon as the brake had left with the delegates, she hurried into the station.

A commotion near the guard's van at once attracted her attention. Someone was supervising the unloading of two huge, oddly-shaped cases with sharp cries and much darting about. It was Mr Mybug; not much fatter, not noticeably otherwise changed, but wearing, instead of the wrinkly pullover and grey bags of yesteryear, an imitation camelhair coat sent from America by *Throw-outs for Britain*, a windbreaker jacket sent from Canada by *Help Britain Again*, British-made sandals smuggled in from Belgium, and corduroy pants lent him by a fellow-traveller.

'Good afternoon, Mr Mybug; how nice to see you again!' said Flora.

Mr Mybug wheeled round, and started back at the sight of her.

'God, this is good,' he said simply, after a pause, taking both her hands and squeezing them as hard as he could (which was not very hard, because of his sedentary habits) and slightly tilting his chin while gazing into her eyes. 'After . . . how many years? But time doesn't matter, does it . . . Flora?'

'You have not changed at all,' said Flora.

'Neither have you, my god,' retorted Mr Mybug earnestly, 'Still the same unawakened, remote, virginal –'

'Someone wishes to speak to you, I think,' Flora murmured, gently withdrawing her hands.

'My dee-ar fellow, der porters are gettink so tough vid my vork,' said a tall man dressed in grey, with gooseberry eyes, a bald head and a very, very sad expression, who was standing at Mr Mybug's elbow. 'Please ask dem to care-haf. After all, it your business is; you der Organizing Secretary are.'

'Of course! Yes! I say, you might be careful there, George; those cases are valuable!' cried Mr Mybug to the two porters.

They took absolutely no notice, but went on manoeuvring the misshapen cases on to a barrow. The man with gooseberry eyes stared sadly at Flora.

'This is Flora Fairford; she's going to help me run this thing,' said Mr Mybug carelessly. 'Flora – Andrassy Hacke. The creator,' and here Mr Mybug reverently lowered his voice and jerked his head towards the cases, 'of *Woman with Wind* and *Woman with Child*.'

'Oh yes. Of course,' said Flora, bowing and smiling to Hacke and hoping the cases would not be opened until she was safely in bed or otherwise out of the way.

'Per-haps Missis Flora doess not der sculpture-art like,' said Hacke in an absolutely furious tone and turning greyish-purple. 'In Inklandt der is no lovink of der Fineart at all. Der artist iss chust so much dunk.'

Flora knew that if she did not instantly pour out a Niagara of adulation this scene would occur every time she ran into Hacke during the coming week, so she at once said loudly:

'I hear endless comments on your work, Mr Hacke; everyone, everywhere, speaks of nothing else; I myself – the wife of a Protestant clergyman in a poor parish with five children to look after – have not yet seen any of it. But I expect I shall see it while I am here. I have so often thought about it since I knew that I was coming to the Conference.'

If a plain woman had said this it might have had no effect, but uttered earnestly by Flora, and conveying as it did both public interest and personal abasement, it succeeded in slightly pacifying Hacke, and fortunately the departure of the train now diverted both gentlemen's attention. A group of what looked like International Thinkers was left standing on the platform, and Mr Mybug, motioning to Flora to follow him, hastened towards them, and one or two of them glanced at him with recognition.

'My god, Mybug, what a journey! I haven't eaten since two,' said a youngish man, good-looking in a blue, battered way, advancing to meet him. 'How do you do,' staring at Flora and bowing slightly.'Are you Flora Fairford? I thought you must be. Did anyone ever tell you you're very like that bust called "Clytie" that used to be in the Roman Room at the British Museum? Girl's head rising out of a stone corolla?'

Flora looked interested, but made no reply.

'Tom Jones, the poet, Flora,' Mr Mybug threw over his shoulder as he entered the group and began introducing himself as the Organizing Secretary and informing the delegates that a brake (for Flora had drawn his attention to the latter) waited in the yard to convey them to Cold Comfort Farm. Flora, by no means wishing to be helpful, but feeling it her duty to be so, now approached three people, two men and a girl who stood slightly on the outskirts of the group.

She was prepared for anything on this trip, and had not

been much surprised to observe, during a recent gust of wind, that under a ragged mink coat the girl wore nothing. She was simply dazzlingly beautiful except for a cross expression and spots, and she had British-made sandals – smuggled in from Lisbon, this time.

One of the men was neatly dressed in grey, with a bald head and gooseberry eyes and a very, very sad expression. He appeared, against the laws of probability, to be ecstatically rubbing all the skin off his shin against a piece of iron girder.

It must be Maser Messe the Transitorist Craftsman, thought Flora. And the other one is surely Peccavi.

Peccavi was pretty old, and he wore ragged shorts, a sun vest striped in blue and white, and sandals. He was completely bald, and looked like a self-conscious and sadistic owl.

Flora smilingly made herself known to the group, and Messe (for it was he) stopped martyring his shin and prepared to accompany her to the brake. But Riska and Peccavi only stared. Peccavi suddenly stood on his head, and the shorts slid down almost to his waist and the blood rushed into his pate. Riska as suddenly spat, and turned away.

'Perhaps they do not understand much English?' Flora said to Messe. 'Mr Mybug speaks a little Portuguese, I believe. Shall I –'

'Zey unnerstan' well enough,' said Messe sadly. 'You notty, notty girl,' shaking his head at Riska. 'It is a challenge among ze Portuguese gipsies,' he added to Flora; 'she sink you want take away her mann.'

'I see. Could you explain to her that I have a man already, *and* five children?'

'She say zat matters not,' translated Messe, after some jabbering. 'She say all women want take away each odder's man. If she see your man, she take him.'

'Then we must take care that she does not see him,' Flora answered pleasantly, thinking what a trial it all was. She smiled at Riska, however, for she did not want to be on embarrassing terms with anyone during the Conference. Riska twiddled her fingers like horns and stuck her tongue out hideously in response, then raced off down the platform after Peccavi.

'*The large utterance of the early Gods.* That's the feeling those two give me,' said Mr Mybug, joining Flora as the whole party moved off towards the exit. He indicated Peccavi and Riska, who were now splashing each other with water from a tank used for the engines. 'Have you noticed how the modern world envies the artist his simplicities? Those two live in a childish paradise of their own contriving. Watch people's faces as they look at them!'

It was true that some of the delegates did look awed and envious, but Flora suspected them of wondering how, and why, Peccavi managed to get such prices for his pictures.

When they came out of the station into the yard:

'I say!' exclaimed Mr Mybug. 'Look at that! It must be the Sort-of-a-Sage from the East.'

Up the hilly road a tall Hindu was striding, with a yellowish-pink turban wound about his magnificent head. His silver beard rippled down to a waist-cloth of the same salmon colour. He was gazing at the dusty road as he walked, and behind him scurried a much smaller and blacker person; his follower, carrying the master's begging bowl and crutch.

The sage drew level with the group in the yard, which was now regarding him curiously; paused, and lifted his arm in greeting.

'Peace,' he said. He looked up. His huge eyes shone with calm light. 'Peace.'

'Peace to you, Teacher,' answered Flora (as everybody else either gaped or looked embarrassed, and one old lady, identified by Flora as Frau Dichtverworren, a psycho-analyst and an early pupil of Freud's, stealthily drew out her note-book and prepared to make notes on the Sage's religious neurosis). 'Welcome to the Conference. You must be tired after your journey. Will you ride with us?'

'No, daughter. This one,' touching his breast, 'and that one,' indicating the follower, 'will walk to the journey's end. That,' glancing at the brake, 'is a device of Monkey.'

'He means the restless, inventive spirit in Man. They call it Monkey. And a dam' good name for it too,' ended Mr Jones moodily, and walked off and stared over a hedge.

'As you will, Teacher,' said Mr Mybug, taking his cue from Flora. 'But I say, you don't know the way, do you?'

'Yes, son. We know the Way. And should we lose our earthly road, I have power to find it again. Farewell.'

He strode off, and the follower, with one fleeting glance from beady eyes at the brake, skimmed after him. It occurred to Flora that he would have liked to ride.

'Power! He means he has the occult power!' It was an ecstatic breath from Mdlle Avaler, the Existentialist. 'Oh, do you think,' turning to Mr Mybug, 'vhat he would read – no, tell? – our fortunes?'

'I *know* he will. He shall – he must!' cried Mr Mybug, overbalancing into the depths of Mdlle Avaler's eyes, which were the colour of the sea in changeable weather. He continued to gaze at her after she had taken her seat beside the prosperous man in the colossal car, with whom she had apparently made acquaintance, and when it drove off (the chauffeur, decided Flora, must have found somebody to tell him the way to the Farm) Mr Mybug was still gazing.

'*C'est la proie à Vénus tout entière attachée,*' misquoted Mr Jones, who had observed what was going on, to Flora. 'Well, are we going to Cold Comfort Farm or are we not, Mrs Fairford? I'm hungry.'

The delegates were now climbing into the brake; and Flora interrupted Mr Mybug's reverie to tell him that she would not accompany them, as she was driving to the Farm with her cousin Reuben.

'Is he still around?' said Mr Mybug. 'All right, Flora; but don't let me down at the other end, will you? These are all V.I.P.s, and we've got to see that they're properly looked after, you know.'

Flora was now pleased that the disgusting subject of money had not been raised between Mr Mybug and herself. She had gathered that he was not gainfully occupied in organizing the Conference, but was doing it from sheer love of Europe's intellectual heritage. Well, she, as unpaid Assistant Organizing Secretary, need not take her duties too seriously. She lightly told him that she would see him some time later, and went off to find Reuben.

3

They drove away through lanes which did not appear to have changed at all in sixteen years, and, save for an occasional poster bearing a portentous green face announcing the Conference on the wall of some shed or barn, the Downs, the fields, and the light in the sky all looked just the same to Flora.

At first Reuben was a little gruff and shy, but they exchanged their news so quickly and with such mutual interest that he was soon at ease, though Flora thought that in repose his face looked even more Starkadderish than formerly.

'And Cousin Amos? Is he still in America?' she asked. 'There is no fear of his coming back and claiming the Farm?'

'Nay, Cousin Flora. No fear o' that. Un's built a gurt church out there, wi' some silly old fule's money. 'Tes called Th' Church o' Th's Quivering Brethren, and un preaches there ivery Sabbath. Us did hear un on th' wireless machine. 'Twas main terrible. Our liddle Nan did weep fer fear.'

'Is Nan a new one? I haven't heard of her.'

'Ay. Now me and Nancy's got our Charley an' our Johnny an' our Ruthie an' liddle Katie an' Rosey an'

Nan. 'Tes a many mouths to feed, surelie,' and Reuben sighed.

'But how is that, Reuben? The last time you wrote the farm was doing well?'

'An' – an' Mrs Beetle, Cousin Flora – do ee mind Aggie Beetle? She do live over at Hangingmere now, along o' Agony Beetle an' Meriam's four byblows – ye mind 'em?' went on Reuben rather hastily.

'Er – yes. Yes, of course. Wasn't she going to have them trained as a dance-band?'

'Ay, but th' Band o' Hope got hold of 'em, and they be all terrible religious. 'Tes a trial to th' poor soul in her old age.'

'It must be. And now, tell me, Reuben – where are all the other Starkadders? You wrote me a line five years ago that they had emigrated to South Africa, and I have heard nothing since.'

Flora paused.

Reuben was silent. What might be described as earth tremors passed over his countenance, but that was all.

'I am sure that something is wrong at the farm, Reuben. Not only do I read it in your face, but I feel it in my bones. And I think you had better tell me what it is,' concluded Flora gravely.

Still he was silent. There was a longish pause.

'At *once*, Reuben,' said Flora, severely.

Reuben, who had been earth-tremoring like mad, now gave a loud groan.

''Tes soon told. *There's no longer Starkadders at Cold Comfort*,' he said.

'What! But, Reuben, there have Always Been Starkadders

at Cold Comfort! What can you mean? Is it because they have all emigrated?'

'All but Urk, an' he's nought but a black stain on us all, wi' his nasty love-drinks an' his meddlin' wi' th' Powers o' Darkness —'

'Never mind Urk now. Tell me about the others.'

''Twere nigh on six years ago, Cousin Flora. Ee knows as how we Starkadders be main violent folk. Some on us pushes others down wells. Some on us bursts our blisters wi' our man's rage. Some on us —'

'I know all that. Seth told me, years ago — as if I couldn't see for myself. I saw his latest picture last week, by the way. He's going bald. But never mind Seth — go on.'

'An' after a while us couldn't niver get on together, wi' the workin' o' the farm.'

'You amaze me,' muttered Flora.

'Time o' th' mustard an' cress harvest theer were a terrible outhees, an' all th' chaps — Micah an' Caraway an' Harkaway an' Ezra an' Luke an' Mark, ay, an' Mark Dolour too — upped an' sailed for South Afriky.'

'Wasn't that a bit rash? I mean, with no prospects or anything?'

'Ee mistakes, Cousin Flora. They did buy a farm out theer. They sees a piece about it bein' up fur sale in a African newspaper what did come round some oranges.'

'I wonder they didn't buy it through a letter from a Gold Coast native. And then what happened?'

'They did lust arter it, Cousin Flora. They could not sleep nor rest. They burns wi' fever an' rages like King David an' Behemoth an' —'

'I can just picture it. Well?'

'So after a main gurt talkin' an' plannin' an' writin' fur advice to Feyther an' Grummer in Ameriky (an' neether o' them e'er sets pen to paper in answer, curses be on 'em both), th' chaps takes all their savin's out o' holes in th' pig-stye wall an' fro' under their beds an' out o' theer Sunday collar boxes, an' they writes off to th' chaps in South Afriky an' they buys Grootebeeste. (That be name o' th' farm in South Afriky, Cousin Flora – Grootebeeste.) An' off they goes, wild an' bedrunk wi' lustful joy.'

'I see. But you stayed behind to look after Cold Comfort.'

'Ay. I do love it dearly here, as ee knows, an' I were as happy as all th' birds o' the' air wi' my Nancy (though un niver will learn ter bake a slaphammock fit ter eat) an' th' liddle bodies-all.'

'Then what went wrong, Reuben?'

'I did sow more n' I could reap, Cousin Flora. There were no labour t' work th' farm wi'. An' then th' weere th' lasses, too.'

'Good heavens! – Prue and Susan and Letty and Phoebe! Are they still here? I imagined them in homes of their own years ago.'

'Ay, an' so uns should be, if th' chaps had not had hearts o' th' Sussex flint and been mad wi' lust for Grootebeeste. As 'twas, there were a turrible outhees.'

Here Reuben paused in his narrative to draw in to the hedge while a large vehicle, half private car and half bus, passed them. It was filled with neat men in grey suits, wearing spectacles, carrying brief-cases, and Biro-penned. They looked all silent and all damned dull. A notice on the car's bonnet read: '*Managerial Revolutionary Party: Delegation to the International Thinkers' Group Conference.*'

The car passed on. None of the Managerial Revolutionary Party's delegates had looked round, and Flora and Reuben were too much absorbed by Reuben's story even to notice them.

'Th' lasses wept an' skreeked like they were beset,' Reuben continued, touching the horse with the whip, 'implorin' th' chaps to take 'em wi' them. But they niver would.'

Flora made no comment. It was difficult to blame the male Starkadders for refusing to take them when one knew the female Starkadders, and difficult to understand the female Starkadders wanting to go when one knew the male Starkadders. The wisest course was silence.

'At last, after hours o' agony, they peerswades th' chaps t' promise to send for 'em all so soon as Grootebeeste be payin' an' prosperin'.'

A fat long time that will be, thought Flora.

'An' off they goes. An' then, an' then – I sweers an oath.'

'Oh dear, Reuben. Now what for?'

'I were driven to it, Cousin Flora. Th' sperrit o' Th' Family did seem to drive me on to do ut. Th' mortsome twilight were fallin', an' far off I hears th' lasses still wailin' on top o' Mockuncle Hill, wheer they'd gathered ter see th' last o' the railway train bearin' th' chaps away to South Afriky. So I sweers that th' lasses should niver know want nor change while I could

> Till th' land
> Wi' th' lone hand.'

'On Aunt Ada's bound copy of the *Milk Producers' Weekly Bulletin and Cowkeepers' Guide.'*

'Ay. How did ee know, Cousin Flora?'

'It was a happy guess. Well, go on. What happened then?'

'Theer's more an' worse to come, Cousin Flora.'

'I wish to hear *everything*, Reuben, please.'

'Ay. An' ee shall. 'Tes comfort to tell ee, somehow. Well, thin I gets in ill-favour wi' Th' Ministry. Th' farm sends up lesser an' lesser haysel, fewer and fewer eggs. Th' milk begins ter dry and th' root crops ter come shrunken —'

'Just as it was when I first came here.'

'Ay. But *then* us could decay away quiet-like, bemongst ourselves. Nowadays, no one maun be let decay, not even if they wants to, seemin'ly. So Th' Ministry begins a-complainin' and a-questionin', and at last they sends down a gennelman from Lunnon.'

'An agricultural expert?'

'Nay, I niver heerd. He were a Mr Parker-Poke. He sets up his bed down at "Th' Condemned Man" (Mrs Murther, honest soul, nigh kills him wi' her cookin' for th' farm's sake, but o' course she dare not finish un off quite), an' ivery day un comes up to th' farm an' de-dottles me wi' advice. There were no peace, an' things did go from bad t' worse. He — he did say as I were niver agricultoorally eddicated.'

'I am very sorry, Reuben.' Flora laid her hand upon her cousin's for a moment. 'No, you are not agriculturally educated; you only know how to make things grow. But go on.'

'At last he did tell me he had written to Th' Ministry. He had told un the old place were no more pratikkle use. He did say as I would niver make a 'fishent farmer. He did tell 'em up theer as I had had ivery chanst. An' so

– an' so, Cousin Flora, he did recommend as I should be gi'en a middock o' land to dwell on wi' me an' mine, an' – an' th' farm itself, th' old place, be – be ploughed under.'

'*Reuben!* My poor cousin!'

'Ee may well say so. An' all th' lads abroad in South Afriky takin' up wi' Grootebeeste (sore evil fell on 'em from th' first day, at that theer Grootebeeste), an' th' lasses half-bedottled wi' pinin' an' grief.'

'But *why* on *earth* didn't you write to them and ask them to come home? They could at least have helped you produce enough swedes and things to satisfy Mr Parker-Poke.'

''Twas me oath, Cousin Flora. Ee knows well that us Starkadders niver breaks an oath. I'd swore to

> Till th' land
> Wi' th' lone hand

an' by that I mun bide. But I were nigh bedott –'

'I feel for you deeply, Reuben, and it has been a great shock to me. I thought everything was going so well. But go on. What happened? Surely the farm has not actually been –?'

'Nay. Un still stands. 'Deed, if un did not know, un would say th' old place looked sonsier an' purtier than her had iver seemed. Look.' And he pointed with his whip downwards along the slope of Mockuncle Hill. At the same time, for they had almost arrived at the farm without noticing, so absorbed were they in their talk, he reined in the horse.

A long, low, irregularly shaped, dazzlingly white building

lay embowered in young trees. Small emerald lawns filled its courtyards. Glowing clusters and bands of flowers stood against its walls. A green banner drooped from the roof on which Flora could just distinguish the words '– *Group Conference*'.

She stared: she turned to Reuben: she stared again.

'Is that –? But it looks – But it can't be, Reuben! It's impossible! It's a cross between a cricket pavilion and a country club!'

'Ay, Cousin Flora. But yon's Cold Comfort Farm, niverth'less,' grimly answered Reuben.

'But who did it? The Ministry?'

'Nay. Didn't I tell ee there was worse t' come? If so be as th' farm had been – been ploughed under, 'twould ha' broke me heart, but at least 'twould ha' been honest grazin' land wheer th' beasts might forage. But as 'tes – well, I'll tell ee. On very day as th' Ministry were a-makin' up its mind over Parker-Poke's letter, a chap did come to see me from Ditchling. He were powerful rich, he says, an' he says he were a Trust.'

'I begin to understand. Was he representing the National Trust?'

'That weren't th' name. 'Twere something about Th' Weavers' Whim. But I mis-remembers. At th' time I were half bedott –'

'Did he offer to buy the farm?'

'That were about it. He says a powerful mort o' money had been left by some wold dead man in charge o' a set o' bodies to buy up wold ancient places what was goin' to be pulled down. They sets 'em to rights, see. Then they hires 'em out for sassieties ter meet in, an' such-like. An' th' money what th' Trust gets for hirin' out the place, they uses to keep th' place all befancied up wi' flowers an' liddle grassy bits an' such.'

'And so you sold it to the Weavers' Whim Trust?'

'I did, Cousin Flora. An' wi' th' money they gi'es me I buys our Ticklepenny's Field an' —'

'Ticklepenny's! I am so glad. Is that where you live?'

'Ay, in th' liddle hut what used to be on th' corner o' Nettle Flitch Field (do ee mind? Meriam th' hired wench did — did often go ter be there). I did move un over to our Ticklepenny's.'

'But what did Mr Parker-Poke and the Ministry say?'

'Un didn't care. Th' Ministry did take tu-third parts o' th' money th' Trust did pay me. They did say as it were compensation. An' I pays them th' other third for our Ticklepenny's.'

'I see. It seems simple enough.'

'Ay, 'twere. It did shut un up, tu. Our Ticklepenny's, look ee, be so goathling an' crow-picken, even th' Ministry won't trouble wi' un. An' Parker-Poke he did go back to Lunnon, brast un fer a bowler-hatten scowkerd!'

'Then where do Phoebe and the others live?'

'In th' Great Barn, Cousin Flora. Th' Trust hev built un liddle bee-cells, like, where un do sleep an' dwell, and uns do eat their meat in th' Great Barn herseln.'

'Don't they do anything to help you at *all*, Reuben?'

'Nay, Cousin Flora. Uns was always poor moithered bodies, as ee may mind.'

Flora did mind. The female Starkadders, as recalled by herself, had always been in some crisis of jam-boiling or jealousy.

'But uns keep th' old place fitty an' scoured for th' Trust, Cousin Flora, an' uns do tend th' liddle flowerets in th' liddle gardens. All they liddle gardens,' pointing with his whip again and then urging the horse forward, 'is wheer th' middens an' th' pigstyes an' th' stables once did be.'

'Are there no animals on the farm now?'

'Nary a horn nor yet an udder, Cousin Flora. Our Big Business were th' last to go. (Ee mind he?) Ah, un had sunk low indeed durin' uns last year here. But 'tes not befittin' that I should tell ee o' that. Ee must find out, or not, as ee pleases, for eeself.'

I jolly well do please, thought Flora.

'I suppose the chaps took him with them to Grootebeeste?' she said.

'Ay. But not before he had shamed us all. Now here we be, Cousin Flora,' as the buggy left the chalk road and the wheels jarred on the flint cobbles of the farmyard. 'Welcome to Cold Comfort agen, mie de-urr. 'Tes sadly changed, to my eyen. But may be ee likes it better so, all clettered an' gaysome as it be?' he ended wistfully.

Flora gazed round: at the artistically lettered sign saying 'The Greate Yarde' swung from a wrought-iron stand; at the green rustic benches outside the windows; at a lot of overfed pigeons rather spoiling the chastity of the general tone; at another notice visible through a door proclaiming 'The Greate Scullerie'; at beds of lavender and plots of borage; at a stone urn –

'Reuben!' Flora stiffened and pointed an accusing finger. 'Can I believe my eyes? There! In that urn!'

Reuben glanced indifferently to where she was pointing.

'Ay, Cousin Flora. 'Tes true. Ee sees what ee sees. It did gi'e me the allovers at first, but now I be used to un.'

'But really, Reuben! Sukebind! Who on earth planted it there?'

'Th' ladies an' gentlemen o' th' Trust. There be a lot more o' un growin' around. They says as these be th' only parts wheer it do grow, and it be a rarity, they says.'

Flora was about to remark, the rarer the better, when Reuben gave a roar of fury. This is more like old times, she thought, but before there was time to question him he darted down some steps leading into a former cellar (now labelled 'The Lytel Store Roome'), and after some scuffling reappeared, hauling with him a small man in a dark suit with a black beard who was clutching a closed woven basket. Pounding after them came an opulent female form tightly covered in red velvet trousers, tweed jacket, flowered turban, and gipsy earings. She was belabouring Reuben's back.

'I say, steady on!' said Flora. 'Need we have this sort of thing?'

Reuben flung the little man on to the turf.

'Lie there, keynard!' he shouted. 'I'll teach ee to swipe th' sely herbs for thy nasty messes!'

The little man gazed up at him silently, with bared teeth.

'Haven't we met before?' Flora was saying to the female form, which was now dusting itself and hauling up its trousers. 'I am Mrs Fairford; I feel sure you must be Mrs Urk Starkadder.'

The hired girl Meriam, for it was she, stared sullenly at Flora, with her mouth open. Flora waited without impatience, for she did not expect that the intervening years had brightened Meriam's wits.

'Ee's face be known ter me an' mine,' said Meriam doubtfully at last. ''Twas in the cards.'

'Was it? How nice! How are you these days? and your mother? and the children – four boys, wasn't it?'

'The cards said as I should meet with a fair woman who would bring trouble.'

'They were mistaken about that, I feel sure; perhaps they had an off-day or something.'

'Ay, they often does. Shockin' chancey, the cards are. Be you innerested in the cards, missus?' and Meriam, with some brightening of expression, unzipped her blouse and spilled a pack of gaudy, greasy cards into her cupped palm. 'Ye've got a lucky face. I'll give yer a two-and-six reading for two-and-tuppence.'

The cessation of a steady grinding sound which had continued in the background throughout her conversation with Meriam now warned Flora that Urk had stopped gritting his teeth, finished replacing the stolen sukebind in the urn under Reuben's direction, and was now taking action stations. She just moved aside in time as he thrust his hairy fist down on Meriam's arm, muttering:

'Come whoam, come whoam, you piece o' dirt. We've no more business here, and I lusts for me cuppa.'

'All right. I could do wi' one meself. Artnoon, Missus Fairford. Don't ferget ter contact me; we'm in th' Brighton phone book – Byewaies, Lechers Lane. Bye-bye!' The last words were uttered in a more or less amiable scream as Urk hauled her away. In a moment Flora saw a very small, filthy dirty car beetling past the gate, and Meriam waved to her as they went by.

'Ee's seen an' heard all me shame now, Cousin Flora,'

said Reuben, pausing beside her as he went to lead away the horse and buggy. 'Th' farm cockered up like a lost woman on Worthing Front, th' chaps abroad in South Afriky, an' Urk Starkadder, as allus kept his wickedness to himself decent-like, settin' up in a Herbal Specialities shop at Bexhill. Ay, an' stealin' th' herbs an' th' flowerets (th' very sukebind itself what you an' me did grub up wi' our own hands, Cousin Flora, off this here land) ter stock it wi'. Wheer's our man's pride, as ee did show us 'twere right ter hev, an' th' poor earth as yet did bear an' keep us in a middock o' bread and a sup o' bracket? Haven't *curses like rookses come home to rest in bosomses and barnses?* Thet they hev; an' rightly so, says you, maybe. An' what do ee think o' Cold Comfort Farm nowadays, Flora Fairford, Robert Poste's child as was? Is ut as ee would see ut, or is ut a blot an' a blannock on th' fair bosom o' Mockuncle Hill? Speak, and speak frank.'

4

But fortunately for Flora (who needed time to reflect upon all that she had heard and seen), the brake containing the delegates, the bus full of Managerial Revolutionaries, and a large hired car crammed with physicists and scientists roaring drunk on anæsthetics, now drove up to the gate. She had only time to say a hasty good-bye to Reuben and to promise to see him again, before hurrying out to welcome the arrivals.

A crowded hour ensued, but it was not disorderly (Mr Jones having taken the precaution of locking the physicists and scientists in their car, where they raved and protested harmlessly enough). Flora and Mr Mybug were provided with lists of names and the rooms allotted, and each delegate was given a numbered key.

Drooping female forms in print gowns and white aprons hurried meekly to and fro bearing cans of hot water and leading delegates to their rooms, but although Flora recognized the sheep-and-hen countenances of Phoebe, Letty and the rest, she was too busy to exchange more than the briefest greeting with them, and even this frightened Prue into hiccoughs. She did observe, however, that they were neater than of yore and that they had not noticeably aged:

this might be due to the lingering influences of her own rehabilitatory work at the farm years ago, to the calmer atmosphere at the farm nowadays, or to the preservative effects of country air and home-made jam.

Not all the delegates were satisfied with their accommodation, for many of them wanted a private sitting-room in which to write reports or paint or hold a salon or go off into trances. Peccavi, for instance, insisted upon having a room overlooking the duckpond. ('He *has* to get into water five times a day,' explained Mr Mybug, who had appointed himself Peccavi's compère. 'Five times – five senses – you get the symbolism? If you give him this room he can just jump out of the window. It's as simple as that.') The Sage (who was discovered by Flora meditating by the old pig-styes, and who looked so conscious, when she asked him how he had possibly managed to cover seven miles as quickly as the cars had done, that she suspected him of using a simple Thibetan magic) refused to sleep in the farmhouse at all, saying that all was illusion, but that while he was Here it was better to sleep beside the humble and unenlightened than beside those utterly in thrall to Monkey. He then walked lightly away, almost seeming to skim over the ground, and confirming Flora's theory about the magic. The follower, who looked exceedingly weary, scurried after him. Flora was not concerned about their comfort, for their values were not those of the other delegates, and she returned to the farm.

She was just in time to catch Mr Mybug dumping his rucksack into the powder-closet opening off Mdlle Avaler's apartment, he observing with a cheery laugh that he was prepared to kip down anywhere. In that case, retorted Flora, he would not mind sharing a shed with his friend Hacke, who was sleeping at the foot of *Woman with Wind* and *Woman with Child*: two Army beds had been set up there, and the gentlemen would be company for one another.

This dealt with, there took place a sharp struggle with Messe over Flora's own room. She had been allotted the smallest, darkest and lowest of those attics into which, in former days, it had not been possible to get at all. But she did not mind, for it was remote from the rooms of all the delegates, and also the topmost boughs of an enormous pear tree were thrusting their abundant leaves and fruit in at the low window. Unfortunately, Messe was avid to martyr himself upon bumpy ceilings and lumpy beds, and Flora encountered him creeping up the attic stairs with an ecstatic expression and his suitcase gripped between his teeth. After an exchange of words, dignified and kind but firm upon her side and tearful upon his, she sent him down again to the airy room and downy bed allotted to him, and returned to her own chamber.

She looked out between the pear-tree boughs. The room gave on the Great Yarde, and below she could see Mr Jones and the large, prosperous man whose car had been outside the station. This was Mr Claud Hubris, representing the views of Democratic Industrial Management at the Conference, and closely identified with the Managerial Revolutionary Party. He and Mr Jones had just unlocked the scientists, who were tumbling out like tigers at a circus. They were all large, vital men, as wild as wild could be, not recognizable as grandsons of that mild and absentminded old scientific josser in *Comic Cuts* who amused the schoolboys of forty years ago. And no one liked them or found them funny any more.

However, Mr Hubris could manage them. He instantly supplied them with drink and promised them a lot of parties, and they all formed themselves into a chain and marched away to their rooms chanting 'The Jolly Physicists':

> 'We care for nobody, no, not we,
> And God knows nobody cares for us.
> Who – was – Britannia?
> Electrons Rule the Waves!'

Then Mr Hubris dusted his hands upon a handkerchief and went off to the Lytel Herbary (formerly a w.c.), which (as Flora could see by craning out of the window) had been fitted up as a bar. Mr Jones mooched about, kicking the cobblestones.

A step caused Flora to turn round. A female form was arranging clean towels upon the basin.

'Phoebe?' said Flora pleasantly, 'I am sure you will remember me; I was Miss Poste.'

'Ay, an' I'm still Miss Starkadder;' retorted Phoebe dejectedly. 'Be you a wife? 'Tes all the luck i' th' tea-leaves some souls do have, surelie.'

Flora wished to learn the state of mind of Phoebe and her relatives, so she went on:

'I hear that you and the other – er – maidens are living in the Great Barn now?'

'Ay – a burden on t' charity o' half-brother Reuben.'

'You must feel it so, I am sure. Do you still do that pretty quilting work?'

'Nay. 'Tes nought but foolishness.'

'Not nowadays. You could sell it to the rich Americans.'

'I wouldna ha' th' heart.'

'Not by yourself, I daresay, and you don't know any rich Americans, but I will give you the address of some people who do,' and Flora wrote upon a leaf torn from one of those successive little notebooks which had accompanied her everywhere since her fifteenth year.

Phoebe stared at it apathetically, but finally put it in her pocket.

Flora then drew from her some account of the other female Starkadders. They seemed in a pretty low way, but fortunately it was negative rather than positive lowness, and she was pleased to hear that they derived most of their pleasure in life from going to church. Having made a note to suggest to the vicar a sermon upon 'Proud Hearts and Idle Hands', she directed Phoebe to bring up to her a tray of supper, for she had decided not to attend the communal dinner on the first evening: the delegates were more than capable of entertaining themselves, and Phoebe and the others would cook and wait at table. She wished to be alone, to think over what she had learned that afternoon.

Evening passed into twilight while she was doing so, and when at last she went downstairs it was night, and the summer moonlight shone through many open windows into the farm. A distant roar, like the Cornish surf only more self-conscious, came from the Greate Laundrie, where the delegates were drinking their coffee, but otherwise all was quiet.

By the bright moonlight Flora wandered from room to

43

room. Her first hours there had been so fully occupied that she had not been able to receive more than a general impression of snowy walls where once rude words had leered out from sooty surfaces, and gleaming floors that were formerly dull and scored by hobnailed boots, and that everything was labelled in wrought iron Greate or Lytel; the Greate Scullerie, the Lytel Rush-dippe Roome, the Greate Staircasee, the Lytel Stille-Roome, the Greate Bedderoome, the Lytel Closete, and so on. But now, observing at her leisure, she hardly recognized some of the shocking old cupboards and filthy cobwebbed alcoves, fitted up as they were with window-seats and oak chests. There were typical farmhouse grandfather clocks ticking all over the place, and where there could have been an expanse of bare wall, it was filled up with a Welsh dresser all over peasant pottery. In the Lytel Scullerie there were fifteen scythes arranged in a half-moon over the sink; there were horse-brasses all round the Greate Inglenooke and all round the Lytel Fireplaces, and Toby jugs and spotted dogs all over the windowsills. The air in the rooms smelt faintly of warm, damp grass: otherwise it was exactly like being locked in the Victoria and Albert Museum after closing time.

Flora ended her tour in that small parlour with faded green wallpaper which had been her favourite refuge during her first visit. She sat down on an oak settle (the tubby little armchairs covered in green repp, the one without arms intended for a lady in a crinoline and the one with arms for a gentleman, had of course gone) and gazed about her. Her spirits felt rather low. The green wallpaper had gone, too, and on the oak panelling thus revealed hung a perfect rash of samplers, with enough alphabets, arks, numerals and cross-stitch trees to stock the entire basement of *The Needlewoman*.

Is it a judgement on the Starkadders because they kept the place in such a mess? she wondered.

Gradually her thoughts were interrupted by a sound like that of someone engaged in eating something, under the open window. Rising, she tiptoed across to it and looked out.

A little elderly man in shabby clothes was sitting immediately beneath the sill with a packet of sandwiches, gazing out across the moonlit Downs. On Flora's giving a cough he turned round, and scrambled to his feet.

'Just havin' a bite. No 'arm intended,' he said in a weak, apologetic voice.

'And no harm done,' Flora replied reassuringly. 'Er – are you on a visit here? Or perhaps you have relatives in Howling?'

She had observed that Mdlle Avaler and Greetë Grümbl, the Swedish Existentialist delegate, wore valuable jewellery, and unidentified visitors must therefore not be permitted to hang about the farm.

'I did 'ave, madam, but 'e must 'ave Moved On. He never answered me p.c.'

'What was his name?'

'Rumbottom, madam. He worked 'ere fourteen years ago, and I thought 'e might still be 'ere. Helping with the spring ungyun harvest, he was. So me first holiday for ten years bein' due to me, I sends Rufie –'

'?'

'Rufus Rumbottom was his full name, madam – a p.c.

45

sayin' I was comin' an' might look 'im up. But if he ain't here, he ain't. Rufie always was a one for change.'

During a pause, Flora observed him more closely – though indeed he was so weedy and meek and small that only his being solitary in the moonlight made him notice-able at all; in a crowd, he would have been part of the background. It occurred to her that the Starkadder maidens might be glad of extra help.

'Would you like to stay here for a week and Help Out?' she asked. 'A lot of very clever ladies and gentlemen are staying here until the 25th, holding a sort of – a kind of –'

'Kind of a Brains Trust,' he nodded, not looking as pleased at her suggestion as she had expected.

'Exactly. We shall need help with the washing-up and things. We can offer seven shillings a day and all found?'

The roar of voices and the snapping of electric switches advancing through the rooms, preceded by odours of cigars and coffee, now warned her that the delegates were about to settle themselves by the Greate Inglenooke in the Greate Laundrie to make a night of it, and she became anxious to make her escape to her bed.

'I beg your pardon?' she said, for the little man had muttered something.

'I says, I come 'ere for a 'oliday.'

'And you will have one, if you stay to Help Out. The work will not be hard, you will have plenty of time off, and the food is ample. If you go to that building labelled the Greate Barne one of the Miss Starkadders will engage you. Tell her that I sent you,' concluded Flora firmly.

The little man touched his bowler and wandered off,

still looking rebellious, and then all the delegates (including the scientists, who were very argumentative and noisy) streamed into the Greate Laundrie, which was situated, as may be remembered, next to Flora's favourite parlour and opened into it.

As she crossed the Greate Laundrie to have a dutiful last word with Mr Mybug before retiring, Flora glanced up at the lintel of the green parlour door. Yes, it was labelled the Quiete Retreate.

Mr Mybug was sitting in a corner with his back to the brilliant throng, sipping boiling black coffee with his eyes shut.

'Mr Mybug,' said Flora in his ear, 'everybody seems to be well entertained and comfortable –'

'Comfortable! God!'

'So I am going to bed. I suggest that you do the same. You seem unwell.'

'You see How It Is with me,' interrupted Mr Mybug, ready, as Flora saw with dismay, for one of his nice long talks all about him. 'How was I to know that This would happen? I didn't want it to happen. It's my accursed Susceptibility. It's not so much that I'm Highly-Sexed –'

'I have no doubt that things will seem very different to-morrow,' soothed Flora, retreating from him so slowly that he did not observe (for he had re-shut his eyes) that she was going, '*Joy cometh in the morning*, you know. *Good night*.'

Having dodged round Riska and Peccavi, who were drawing black magic symbols on the floor of the dim Greate Kitchene and gibbered absently at her as she passed, she made her way upstairs to her room, which smelled of cool leaves, and retired to rest.

Some hours earlier Reuben's Nancy, opening the back door of their hut to pour away the tea-leaves and show little Nan the rising moon, was startled to see a tall, half-naked form seated beside a flickering fire on the doorstep. A smaller, squatting dark figure instantly extended to her an empty bowl.

'Evenin' to ee,' said Nancy at last, as neither figure spoke.

'Peace,' replied the Sage, without raising his eyes.

The follower did not speak but continued to hold out the bowl.

'Thou wilt give this one,' touching his breast, 'and that one,' indicating the follower, 'their evening meal, daughter,' said the Sage at last, 'oil and fruit and rice are required.'

The follower's eyes glittered like cut-steel beads, and he pushed the bowl nearer, only to be rebuked by a look from his master.

'That I wull,' Nancy answered cheerfully. 'Nan, lovey, run in an' get th' butter off th' table, an' a handful o' cobs out of th' nut basket, an' two o' ee's liddle fists full o' barley from th' crock. Put un in th' bowl as th' gennelman be holdin' out to ee.'

When Nan returned with the full bowl, the follower snatched it, then scooped up the tea-leaves from the earth with a scallop shell from the garden border and set it aside as if for himself.

'Don't ee, now don't ee eat that mook, dear soul; 'twill give ee th' goodness-knows!' exclaimed Nancy. 'Nan, run in agen an' bring un out a slice o' bread an' th' beef dripping.'

But no sooner had the follower held the bread to his

nose, which he did eagerly enough, than he swooned. An expression of horror was fixed upon his face, and his feet were almost in the fire.

His master took no notice, so Nancy, having removed his feet to safety, tried to revive him with the tea-leaves and water; when this proved useless, all the children, who had crowded to the door, began to cry, and Reuben, who had just returned home, rushed out in a rage.

They slapped the follower's feet, they waved his arms up and down, they burned feathers under his nose: in vain. At last Reuben, who wanted his supper, addressed the Sage:

'I be wounded to disturb ee, sir, but perhaps ee could bring un's friend round?'

At the third repetition the Sage looked up. 'All is illusion,' he said, and looked down again.

'Holy thoughts be all very well while un's friend is dyin', belike,' muttered Reuben, but at that instant the follower uttered a deep sigh, sat up, and, pouring out the barley, began to grind it in a little hand mill which he drew from a recess within his scanty robes.

'Be danged to ee for a chap,' said Reuben crossly, and went in and slammed the door.

5

In the morning, when Nancy opened it, she found a third figure seated upon the step – a small man in dark clothes and bowler hat.

'Just havin' a bit of a warm. No offence meant,' he said, and touched the hat. 'The young lady up the farm give me a posh bed, but it suits me better down 'ere, don't it, chum?' to the follower, who salaamed, but did not answer.

'And welcome,' answered Nancy.

She thought that Reuben might send all three of them packing, but meanwhile she was too kind to do it herself, and there was the breakfast to cook, so she went indoors.

This was Monday, and the Conference officially opened to-day. A programme of activities had been prepared by Meutre, President of the International Thinkers' Group, and a copy given to each delegate and to Mr Mybug and Flora: the latter's breakfast had been rendered tastier by the news, conveyed to her by Mr Claud Hubris, that Mrs Ernestine Thump had contacted him by telephone late last night and was coming down for the inside of the week and would want a bed.

The morning was to be devoted to Individual Discussions between the delegates, and the afternoon to the promulgation of a Bill of Human Rights, drawn up after the delegates had suggested what such rights should be, and promulgated by Mr Claud Hubris at a meeting in the Greate Kitchene.

There was a rather painful scene after breakfast with the very old Liberal delegate, Mr Gonn. He became breathless with excitement on hearing about the Bill of Human Rights, freely using the words 'superb' and 'epoch-making', and at one point crying and having to be supplied with a handkerchief by Flora, as he was too poor to possess any of his own. He seemed to be suffering from the delusion that the promulgation would have practical results, and it took Flora and Mr Jones almost an hour to convince him that so far as Mr Claud Hubris and the other people with the power were concerned, it was not even a parlour game.

'He says that when he was young, such expressions as "Bill of Human Rights" were not used except with "high seriousness and practical intent",' said Flora, as she and Mr Jones watched Mr Gonn tottering sadly away in the aimless, unplanned style that was already irritating the Managerial Revolutionaries.

'Why wasn't there honey for breakfast?' demanded Mr Jones, dismissing Mr Gonn and his intentions. 'I crave for honey. It stimulates certain glands in me.'

Flora refrained from suggesting that in a previous incarnation he might have been a bear, though in her opinion more than vestigial ursine traces still lingered in him.

They were seated upon a bench under the windows in the yard, to which sunny place Flora had retired with ten pounds of peas to shell for luncheon; an occupation she had chosen for herself as being most likely to keep her away from delegates.

Mr Jones now sank down upon the warm stones, put his head on his arms in silence, and began to turn grey in the face.

This will never do, thought Flora.

'Will you help me with these?' she said, holding up a pod.

'My dear girl,' gritted Mr Jones, with an awful laugh, 'I am a poet, not a *suburban helot*.'

'I am sure you could, if you tried; it is not difficult,' replied Flora, unruffled, and after a minute and a half or so, filled with snortings and caracolings suggestive of a self-conscious horse, Mr Jones did scoop up some peas and make a start.

'Who is that?' asked Flora in a lowered tone, as a large red scientist walked by, bellowing with laughter in the ear of a small yellow scientist.

'The big one? Farine, the *Inconceivable Frameworks* man. In the lab. he works with incredibly delicate instruments, and out of it he relates incredibly indelicate anecdotes.'

'Oh.'

'As husband and father, if you care to know, he is chancy. He has also discovered a gas which is absolutely no use at all.'

'What a shame. And who is that with him?'

'O. E. Cumulus. Nothing *he* has ever discovered is any use, either.'

'I see.'

'There was a suggestion at one time that Cumulus should be made President of the Milk Nature Dry Society –'

'I don't think I remember?'

'Dear Flora Fairford, where have you lived? It was a movement to *wrench* the Old Girl's last secrets out of her and *force* her to make us all comfortable and happy – you must have heard about it on the air. But the Committee decided that he hadn't enough empirical drive for the job.'

'Who did get it, then?'

'W. W. R. Token. He went slap through chemical fertilizers and artificial insemination, and came out the other side in the middle of Virgil's *Georgics*. It's all there, he said. Everything we want to know.'

'I seem to remember the posters.'

'Yes. *Farmers! Let Publius Vergilius Maro tell you how!* But it didn't work. Nothing ever works. Why? Why? All we want,' said Mr Jones, rolling listlessly over and crushing half a pound of perfectly sound peas, 'is to be comfortable and happy, curse us all. But none of us are. Why?'

'Well,' began Flora – cautiously, for this was delicate ground – 'surely some people –'

'Yes, the mother-fixation boys with bank balances typifying their anal neuroses, the tillers of worm-deserted suburban plots, the growers of piddling lettuces and obscene tomatoes, the sly, shapeless bodies on which the sun never strikes!'

'Some of them do belong to bicycling clubs –'

'Darting like gutless fish through the dim poisoned sluices of the cities!' cut in Mr Jones – rather neatly, Flora thought, but she only added –

'And swimming clubs, too.'

'And bowls and half-pints and darts! God, how I loathe darts!' shrieked Mr Jones, leaping up and shedding peas in all directions. 'The rats with Post Office Savings books! The lice with families! The smug weazels who become doctors and bishops and admirals!'

'Well, really, Mr Jones, if nothing and no one existed, what would you write poetry about?' said Flora with decision. 'I do not wish to distress you further, but the world is here, you know, and you are in it. You may not like it –'

'Like it! Hahahahaha! Do you know' – shaking a blue finger at her – 'that when Peccavi (now he *is* a free spirit) heard that O. E. Cumulus is "devoted" to his wife and family, he burst a *BLOOD*-vessel?'

'Was it a large one?' There was an uncontrollable note of hope in Flora's tone.

'No. Quite a small one,' answered Mr Jones sulkily, after a pause.

'I hope he is better now,' said Flora, recollecting herself. 'He must be, or he couldn't always be jumping into the duck pond with Hacke.'

Mr Jones only nodded moodily and lounged away, leaving Flora to finish the peas.

This she did undisturbed, except for one occasion when Mr Mybug passed by, saying earnestly to the old psychoanalyst Frau Dichtverworren:

'But surely analysis would help Mdlle Avaler to control the fearful power which she has over m-er-over men?'

'Your young friendt likes to be as she iss,' replied Frau Dichtverworren, with a smile which overwhelmingly suggested to Flora the Wolf Paddock at Whipsnade. 'Zo, we cannot help. Before God died (your young friendt iss Existentialist, und she vould say that He iss dead) He would sometimes help peoples against der vill. Or so dey said. Ve

54

are not God. Ve cannot do zo. Ve can only help dem to do little zings with what dey haf. For mostly,' ended Frau Dichtverworren, settling her stiff linen cravat with another Whipsnade smile, 'dey haf not much.'

Flora listened with interest. For her part she was inclined to like Mdlle Avaler, who displayed in her blouses of fragile snowdrop lace and her combs of pale tortoiseshell the adorable French genius for elegant detail, and who had not so far embarrassed Flora with confidences or complaints. She was gifted with two slightly projecting teeth which lifted her upper lip like a pink bud, and, as if this were not enough, Heaven had dowered her with a difficulty in pronouncing the letters 'th'.

Luncheon was served in the Greate Laundrie, and Flora, who thought it only polite, as well as her duty, to put in an occasional appearance at the meals and the *symposia* and *conversazioni*, was present. A portable microphone had been installed in the Greate Laundrie for the benefit of those delegates whose importance in the Scheme of Things made it impossible for them to be kept in ignorance of each day's toll of smashes, crashes and bashes, and Flora's enjoyment of her first forkful of peas was tempered by an announcement, made in a silky, disdainful voice, about the remains of two eighty-year-old female twins who had flown the Pacific at four hundred miles an hour having been hauled out of a coral lagoon by a Samoan fisherman. No one took any notice except, presumably, the relatives of the eighty-year-old female twins.

After luncheon the delegates began to assemble in the Greate Kitchene, and while Flora was wandering about, glancing at the furnishings and growing more certain with every hour that a new task lay before her at the farm, she heard a voice which seemed familiar shouting away at the far end of the room. She glanced across. Yes, it was Mrs Ernestine Thump (hat, as usual, by Manqué et Cie), talking to Mr Hubris. Flora crossed the room and approached her.

'How do you do, Mrs Thump. Would you like to see your room?'

'Yes, yes, here I am,' shouted Mrs Thump; 'but I can't stay longer than Friday by an early train, and I'm only fitting this in between a sitting of the W.F.A.A. Committee and a Constituents' Rally at Little Drinking! Well, *you* look fitter than when we last met,' surveying Flora, 'but of course the air's getting better everywhere since We took over! We like to keep in touch with intellectual doings, you know, and this Bill of Human Rights is right in line with Our planned co-ordination of industrial and agricultural activities. Personally, I look forward to an epoch when there shall no longer exist one square inch of unplanned, un-coordinated soil on the Globe! Ha! they're going to begin! Come On!'

However, Flora permitted Mrs Ernestine Thump to bound away into a seat opposite Mr Claud Hubris, while she herself took one conveniently near the door. On one side she had no neighbour; on the other was Mr Jones, still bearing on his countenance traces of the start of horror he had given upon first catching sight of Mrs Ernestine Thump. He offered Flora a boiled sweet, which she declined.

Mr Claud Hubris, the Managerial Expert to end Managerial Experts, now rose to address the delegates. He was surrounded by members of the Managerial

Revolutionary Party; supervising technicians, operating executives, and technological unemployment statistical research workers, all of whom sat with their neat, spectacled faces turned idolatrously towards him. The rest of the delegates looked pretty glum, and Mdlle Avaler, Flora observed, looked disrespectful.

'Ladies and gentlemen,' Mr Claud Hubris began in a quick, fruity voice, smilingly flashing his glasses over the assembly, 'we are here this afternoon to draw up, by means of that system of democratic discussion for which this island is globally famous, a Bill of Human Rights. Whatever our political views may be' (Mr Hubris himself had no political views; he did not need them; he had enough power without) 'I am sure that we are all agreed upon one fact: Man's potentialities are enormous and still largely untapped.'

Here all the supervisory technicians, superintendents, and administrative engineers clapped like mad, and the two Professors of Genetics, Breed and Brood, stamped with their feet, but Mdlle Avaler whistled through her teeth, as a French audience does when it dislikes an actor.

'Largely untapped,' repeated Mr Hubris. 'In physics' (frenzied clapping and hysterical laughter from Professors Farine, O. E. Cumulus and W. W. R. Token), 'in the science of improving livestock' (more feet-stamping from Professors Breed and Brood) – 'in every branch, in fact, of applied scientific research, Man is on the up and up. Nothing, ladies and gentlemen, can stop us. We are on the up and up, and up-up-up we shall go!'

Flora thought this very likely.

'To quote the words of the late script-writer

Shape-of-Things-to-Come Wells,' continued Mr Hubris, when the thunderous applause had died away, '*Man is Master In His Own House.*'

'He has ve brokers in!' cooed Mdlle Avaler, with a maddening toss of her head.

Mr Hubris darted her an indulgent glance, and resumed: 'Now as to the Rights of the Human Race (shall we call it The Consumer? for it is in this aspect of its functions that we are fundamentally concerned with it), they are three.' Mr Hubris paused, and tried to make his huge face look humane while he ticked off the three on his huge white fingers. 'Nutriment, Employment, Domicile. The ladies,' and here the face suddenly slipped alarmingly into a kind of smile, 'would no doubt say that The Consumers (as we have agreed to call The Human Race) have also a right to Love.' (A faint wolf-howl from Mr Jones, of which no one took the slightest notice.) 'We concede that, of course. But Love is not an Essential. The Consumers cannot continue to function without Nutriment, Employment and Domicile, but, they *can* continue to function without Love. The same is true of art and beauty and nature and religion (except of course as nature is useful to The Consumers) and all that sort of thing. Very nice, no doubt. Very pleasant, no doubt. Very useful, in some cases, no doubt; they can all be employed in advertising. But NOT, ladies and gentlemen, NOT ESSENTIAL.

'Now let us take Nutriment first,' went on Mr Hubris, smiling round on the assembly like a jaguar. 'I speak with authority here in my capacity as Acting Technical Adviser for Nutritional Necessities Inc., which has branches all over the Globe. My Corporation supplies substances containing sufficient calorific content to sustain life on a reasonable basis, and when I say that The Consumers have a *right* to such substances, I must of course qualify that statement by emphasizing that only those members among The Consumers who can *pay* for nutritional substances have a *right* to them. In other words, *Nutritional Necessities Inc. will always sell to a buyer.'*

'Hear, hear,' cried Mrs Ernestine Thump, and Manqué et Cie's hat fell over one glistening little eye.

'For other Corporations, of course, I cannot speak. Indeed,' and once more Mr Hubris's teeth became visible to his fascinated audience, 'now I come to think of it, I doubt if there *are* any other corporations. Nutritional Necessities Inc. has seen to that, vertically *and* horizontally. Nut: Nes: Inc: has ricefields in Dakota and soya-fields in Indo-China, acres of orchards in Italy, and drained fjords full of edible lichen in Norway. *Wherever the digestive process is at work, there Nut: Nes: Inc: has been at work.* That is our boast. We are also in close touch with the Ministry. They buy from us. That is why you, ladies and gentlemen, are regularly supplied with sufficient calories to sustain life on a reasonable basis.'

There was another prolonged burst of applause, through which Mr Jones was heard to mutter: *Suppose you want it on an unreasonable basis?*

'And believe me, ladies and gentlemen,' said Mr Claud Hubris, suddenly going grave, while a chilly cloud seemed to pass over the surface of his glasses, 'it is a good thing. It is a much better thing. Waste, planlessness, all the uneconomic muddle of Nature – drought, flood, glut and scarcity – are all going to be done away with by Nut:

Nes: Inc:. In the words of our Motto, *God Knows How But We Know Better.*'

The applause that followed this was tremendous, and O. E. Cumulus fell under his chair, and had to be hauled up by Professor Farine. When it had ceased, Mr Hubris resumed, with what was intended for a sunny, reassuring smile:

'So have no fear, ladies and gentlemen. The Race has a Right to Nutriment. Good! Nutritional Necessities Inc. will see to it that the Race never quite starves. Now as to Domicile. Domicile is generally admitted –'

Here, as a wasp had flown in through an open window and was harrying the delegates in Flora's vicinity, and as she had been aware for some time of slight sounds proceeding from the supposedly unoccupied Lytel Scullerie next door, she made off in pursuit of the wasp and escaped from the room.

Having inhaled some fresh air, she looked round the Lytel Scullerie. The cool, whitewashed walls and stone floor, the enormous stone copper and equally enormous plate-rack of smooth, sodden wood, presented a peaceful appearance. All was now silent and as usual; except that tethered to the peckle-post in the miniature garden outside (formerly a cow-yard) was an exceedingly fat cow with only three legs, whose large eyes were almost closed as she munched her way through a clump of choice delphiniums.

Flora looked at the copper. No one could get behind that. Then she looked into the dim corner by the plate-rack. Something appeared to be grubbing about there in the shadows, and, even as she saw it, a piping voice began:

'Ay, 'tes lost and gone for ever, my treasure, my mippet. Curses on th' black-hearted jealousboots as stole it from me all they years ago! Their fault will come whoam to 'em – ay, it *has* come whoam, for they be all scattered abroad in foreign partses, leavin' their maidies desolate, and th' farm be all dolled up like an ailin' cow's dinner. Ay, the beastses, they knows! Nary a pig in sight, nor yet a cockerel nor sheepses. 'Tes enough to break a man's heart, if he had not laid up a two-room cottage wi' three acres o' ground for himsel', wi' our Mistrust an' our Mislay an' our Mishap an' our Misdemeanour all up at Howchiker Hall (blessin's on 'er stately gowden head, my Lady Elfine!). Nay, 'tes not here, my lost treasure, and I mun away home again to Howchiker.'

And out of the shadow came a little, very old man dressed in a white smock, and a cowherd's hat largely composed of shreds of material held together by thorns. He wore laced boots and leggings and leant on a crooked stick.

'Adam Lambsbreath!' exclaimed Flora, pleased to see him, though he and she had never been favourites of one another's. 'Why, I thought you were –'

She checked herself, but it was too late.

'Ay, Robert Poste's child,' nodded Adam, scowling and resting his hands on his stick. 'Ye thought I were dead. But I bean't. See ee?'

'Yes, I do. I'm sorry.'

'Sorry I bean't dead? Out on ee for a shameless heart o' flint! Sich words in a man's face!' and he shook his stick at her.

'No, no, of course I didn't mean that. I am pleased to

61

see you again, Adam.' (She just prevented herself from saying something about old faces, and hurried on): 'Er – it's a long time since we met, isn't it? I suppose you are still up at Haute-Couture Hall with Lady Hawk-Monitor?'

'Ay, an' like to be, Robert Poste's child.'

'Has she returned yet? I understand that the family was expected home from America this week.'

'Ay, Robert Poste's child. They'm all whoam: they come o' Sattidy. But my Lady Elfine she's still wild as a marsh-tigget. 'Tes not seemly for th' mother o' three gurt lads and four sonsy lasses to ride creerin' round th' landscapes on a horse.'

'What were you looking for just now?' Flora went on, and she leant comfortably back against the copper, at the same time giving a gentle push to the Lytel Scullerie door. It swung slowly to, and the sound of Mr Hubris's voice grating on about Domiciles was reduced to a distant ululation suggesting a flying bomb that never came any nearer.

'Me liddle mop,' Adam answered. 'Her as I did hev many a long year, hangin' above t' gurt old greasy washin'-up bowl.'

'I remember.' Flora decided not to remind him that it was she who had given him the little mop, a fact which he had apparently forgotten. 'How did you come to lose it? Surely you took it when you and the cows went to live at Haute-Couture Hall?'

'So I did. So I did, Robert Poste's child. But there was them still livin' at Cold Comfort as bore me malice in their black heartses, and 'twas them as did steal un from me.'

'I say, what a shame! What did they do with it?'

62

'Nay, how should I know, Robert Poste's child? One says a-one thing, one du say a-nother, to be-dottle me, like. Some says as Mus' Ezra, afore he went off to South Afriky, did fling un down th' well up in Ticklepenny's.'

'Too bad. The well is still working, then?' asked Flora, pleased to hear of something remaining as it used to be.

'Nay. 'Tes all filled up.'

'What on earth for, Adam?'

'Nay, how should I know? Foolishness, belike.'

Flora, too, thought that this was probably the explanation.

A pause now ensued. Adam poked with his stick in the copper, and Flora gazed dreamily through the further door at the cow, who had begun upon a bed of choice carnations. The door of the Lytel Scullerie slowly blew open again in the breeze, and Flora heard

'– governed by his rating as a socially productive unit, which indicates his integration within the social –'

before she pushed it to again.

It suddenly occurred to her that the cow's face was familiar.

'That cow is very like Feckless, Adam. Is she a relation?' she said, wondering if it would be any use asking him to call her Mrs Fairford.

'Ay,' muttered Adam, still poking about in the copper with his back to her. 'But our Feckless, she'm lyin' in th' churchyard mould, Robert Poste's child, wi' th' liddle Live-and-Let-Live blossoms grow'n over un's grave. Ay, near broke my heart, it did, when our Feckless were took.'

63

'I am sorry. I hope she was not ill for long?'

'A matter o' six weeks. Not that it were an illness. 'Twere more a shock to her sperrits.'

'She always was sensitive,' said Flora, wishing to soothe him. 'I remember her well.'

'Ay. An' Big Business, he were a – a close friend o' our Feckless's, if ee do remember that tu?'

Flora nodded.

'Big Business an' Feckless an' our Graceless an' our Pointless an' our Aimless, they was all close friends. Fair managed un all, Big Business did, an' they looked up to he. Yon,' and he nodded towards the cow, 'yon's our Feckless's great-granddaughter.'

'Really? How very interesting! But she's not so pretty as Feckless was.'

'Nay, nor niver could be, Robert Poste's child. Do ee mind how our Feckless did perk up when Mus' Reuben did become measter o' th' farm an' did gie un a plenty to eat?'

'Yes indeed,' replied Flora. She remembered nothing of the sort, but it had suddenly occurred to her that Adam might know the secret of the shame that Big Business had brought upon the Starkadders and the farm, which Reuben had mentioned.

'What did upset Feckless, after you had all gone to live at Haute-Couture Hall?' she went on. 'Was it something to do with Big Business?'

Adam had now almost disappeared inside the copper, where he was still busily raking with his stick, but she could see the back of his neck, and it was almost as red as his spotted kerchief.

'Nay, Robert Poste's child. Ay; ay, 'twere. But it were somethin' as be most unbefittin' to mention to a maidy.'

'But I bean't – I mean, I'm not a maidy any more. I am Mrs Charles Fairford, and I have five children.'

'Why couldn't ee say so befirst?' snapped Adam, coming hastily out of the copper. 'Our Feckless did pine away for shame 'cause our Big Business did – did lend hisself out to th' scientific gents.'

'?'

'Ay. Fur increasin' th' goodness o' th' livestock i' these parts – ay, an' in South Afriky, too, I hears.'

'I understand,' replied Flora, with reserve.

'Ay. Th' scientific gents did come round a-speerin' an' a-pleadin', an' Mus' Micah an' Mus' Reuben (I were here at th' time, a-seekin' fur me lost treasure, an' I hears what they says wi' th' tears nigh runnin' down their false, black-hearted faces). Solemn-like they speaks, as if they were i' church though they be only standin' an' jawin' by th' old duck-pond, an' Mus' Micah an' Mus' Reuben all be-swole i' th' face wi' rage, but sayin' niver a word.'

'If they disapproved so strongly, why did they ever let Big Business go?'

''Twas th' black-hearted Ministry as did send th' scientific gents to Cold Comfort; an' who dare say th' Ministry nay? Ay, an' th' gents did be-dottle Mus' Micah an' Mus' Reuben wi' flatterin'. They says they has a *Awful Responsibility*. (I hears 'em.) *Reely superior beastses* (they says, argyfyin'-like) *should spread their influence*. An' what wi' th' Ministry an' what wi' bein' puffed up wi' vanity, Mus' Reuben an' Mus' Micah they lets our Big Business go. An' 'twere the shame o' it (him havin' kept his affairs

private up till then) as did break our Feckless's lovin'
heart.'

'And where is he now?'

'In South Afriky, so I hears. Whin he did come whoam
here after his journeyin's, Mus' Micah an' th' rest did take
him off to that theer Grootebeeste, th' Lord preserve him.'

'Perhaps it was as well. I don't quite know what a bull
would do with himself at Cold Comfort nowadays.'

'Them's true wordses, Robert Poste's child. 'Tes more
like th' Vicarage on Garden Party day, bean't it? 'Tes flyin'
in th' face o' Natur', I says.'

'My own view exactly.'

'Ay, an' takin' off our Big Business on yon scientific
work were flyin' in th' face o' Natur', too. Very worst flyin'
in th' face o' Natur' as iver I heerd on, *that* were. Why,
Robert Poste's child –'

'Yes, but never mind that now. Shall we walk up to
Ticklepenny's Corner? We might look into the well, to
see if your little mop is down there?' For Flora judged
from the enthusiasm of the latest burst of applause that
the promulgation of the Bill of Human Rights was almost
over, and she wished to avoid delegates hurrying out in
search of admiration and tea.

But Adam hesitated. Doubt and suspicion chased one
another across the morbific crevasses of his facial terrain.

'What is the matter?' Flora enquired patiently.

'Belike ee harbours some fearsome plot agin me an' mine?'

'I assure you I don't. I'm far too busy.'

'There be allus time an' to spare for wickudness.'

'Have it your own way, but I do think you might take
a sporting chance on it.'

'I'll walk wi' ee if so be as ee goes a-front o' me an' our Mishap,' said Adam at last, untethering the cow (who was just finishing some selected alpines) and motioning Flora on with his stick.

'Done!' cried Flora, and they set off.

Guided by peevish cries from the old cowman, Flora avoided the usual path up to Ticklepenny's, and crossed the meadow which ran transversely across the base of Mockuncle Hill. It was windy here on the rising wolds, and her voluminous skirts billowed as she climbed, while Adam plodded behind at a good pace, and, in spite of her handicap, Mishap managed nicely.

As they came out on to the uplands leading on to Ticklepenny's, they heard hoofs thudding up behind them on the turf, and Flora turned. Four riders were approaching. Mishap gave a low moo of welcome, and the lady on the large black stallion who led the party waved her crop in greeting. In another moment she drew rein beside Flora.

'Darling!' she exclaimed, stooping to press her cool, sweet-smelling cheek to Flora's own.

It was Elfine.

''Heard you were here,' she said, with the trace of former gruffness which always returned to her voice when she was moved or shy. ''Been simply longing to see you. I say, *can* you come to dinner tonight? Just me and the sons – the husband will be at a J.P. meeting – oh, these are the sons. Hereward – Torquil – Peregrine' – indicating them with her crop. 'This is Flora Fairford. You know – my best friend,' she ended gruffly.

The three handsome boys on dapple grey cobs said, 'How do you do, Mrs Fairford,' and fixed their eyes, keen and sparkling above hard, blooming cheeks, upon Flora's face. She herself surveyed Elfine with affectionate satisfaction.

Her complexion had not suffered from the central heating of Washington mansions, her form was still as nymph-like, her eyes still as sapphire, but the springing golden mane that Flora had once taught her to subdue was now coiled into a Diana-knot of faultless structure and gloss, while her habit fitted *à merveille*, and her gloves, boots, and hat were perfect of their kind.

However, as she straightened herself after embracing Flora, a slim volume fell from her skirt pocket. Forestalling the boys, who all three leapt from their saddles, Flora returned it to her with a smile: it was John Greenleaf Whittier's poem *Snow-bound*. Lady Hawk-Monitor crimsoned.

'The Mother reads poetry,' said Peregrine defiantly.

'Such frightful poetry, too,' said Torquil.

'All poetry is frightful,' drawled Hereward, who wrote it himself and who was his mother's favourite.

'Can you come, dear Flora? Do,' said Elfine.

Flora regretfully explained that her evening duties kept her at Cold Comfort until after dinner, but it was arranged that she should go to drink coffee at Haute-Couture Hall at half-past eight on the following evening, and Elfine then apologized that she must ride home at once to take tea with the daughters, Naomi, Rachel and Esther. ('Jews never call their young by those adorable soft Bible names, do they?' she observed, 'and *someone* has to.')

Flora accompanied the party to the summit of Mockuncle Hill, walking amidst the horses' damp, glossy flanks and breathing the warm air which they threw off while she talked with her friend.

'How are you liking the Conference, darling? Loving it, I expect; you're so clever.' Elfine's fond eyes dwelt respectfully upon her face.

Flora replied (with caution, for she did not wish to unsettle Lady Hawk-Monitor's awe of clever people) that the Conference was much what she had expected. She then added that she was far from satisfied with the state of Cold Comfort Farm.

'But, ducky, why? It's all so lovely and tidy nowadays. I should have thought you would have *madly* approved.'

Flora admitted it. Nevertheless, she shook her head.

'You'll have to have a word with the husband. *He* says Cold Comfort is all wrong. Of course it was such a mistake the he-cousins going abroad,' said Elfine.

'I suppose there is no chance of Aunt Ada coming home?'

'Not one chance, I should say. She adores Hollywood. When she writes to the young every year on their birthdays she always says she's *never* coming home.'

'She must be – how old, Elfine?'

'Flora, nobody knows. I daren't think about it, myself. She always wears white, you know, and whacking great sapphires. And *every* night she's at a party!'

Flora shuddered (at the parties, not at Aunt Ada Doom's gay old age) and dismissed the idea that she might be induced to return and manage the farm once more. Then, having bidden an affectionate farewell to Elfine and watched the riders and Adam and Mishap vanish over the brow of Teazeaunt Beacon, she walked home at her ease, looking at the view and hoping that she would not encounter Mr Mybug or Mr Jones.

At Ticklepenny's Corner she paused to inspect the well. It was fitted up with a fancy arch, a lid, a stone seat carved with a bit of poetry about wells in Gothic letters, and a Crafty statue of a saint who was evidently O. C. Wells. In fact, there was everything at the well except water, for when Flora dropped a stone into it nothing came up but a dry 'chink' and rather a whiff.

She shook her head as she stepped down from the stone seat. Something would have to be done, and if she were not soon approached by Reuben with a plea for help, she must set about doing something without Reuben's aid.

The next evening the plea came.

But on this fine Monday evening, when the only object marring the smug prettiness of Cold Comfort Farm was Reuben's tumbledown cottage at the corner of Ticklepenny's tilted, flinty field, the delegates (some bloated with sandwiches and tea and others prevented by their private woes from relishing either) were strolling along the wolds to gaze at the spacious view across the Downs, and obtain a glittering glimpse of the far-off sea.

'There! Now us canna hev our tea wi' th' door open!' exclaimed Nancy, as Mr Claud Hubris hove in sight, accompanied by a swarm of little Managerial Revolutionaries, for the way to the vantage point ran past the cottage's rear. 'Niver mind, liddle souls. Come Sunday they-all 'ull be gone. Rosey Starkadder, did I see ee put out's tongue at yon? Fur shame! I doan' wanna tell Feyther o' ee.'

'Feyther did shake un's fist at yon.'

'Ay, he's allus a-doin' of it,' put in Charley, Reuben's eldest.

''Tes defferent for Feyther. Now eat up tea, an' let's hear no more.'

Unfortunately, the sage and the follower and the helper-out also took their evening meal at this hour, and for some of the delegates their humble arrangements possessed all the charms of novelty, there invariably being a point at which intellectuals weary of their own fleshpots and feast of reason and flow of soul, and come poking desolately amidst the tea and fried herrings prepared for themselves by unintellectuals. Mdlle Avaler, Peccavi, Riska and Mr Mybug now strolled up to Nancy's back doorstep and stood gazing at the party seated thereon.

'I say, my father, why don't you put in an appearance at any of the lectures?' presently said Mr Mybug, to the Sage. 'Aren't you supposed to be representing Higher Thought?'

'Peace,' answered the Sage, after a long pause and without looking up.

Poor Mr Mybug had not one clue to this, so he made a mental note to complain about the Sage's extraordinary lack of public-spiritedness to Meutre, the I.T.G.'s President.

'To sit on ve ground! To eat rough food! To be good!' sighed Mdlle Avaler. 'How delicious – and how it is impossible!'

'Your painter friend seems at home with them,' observed Mr Hubris, pausing in his promenade with the Managerial Revolutionaries that one of them might stand on tiptoe before him to light his cigar.

'Of course. He's the simplest person imaginable – a child, a savage, at heart,' snapped Mr Mybug.

Peccavi had finished bolting the helper-out's kipper, and had begun upon an exiguous cache of winkles collected that morning from the seashore by the follower. The latter could not protect them, as he was fully occupied with Riska, who (clad only in one of the many types of military jacket which Recent Events have left for sale at reduced prices) was tickling his soles with a twig. He, silent with fear, crouched motionlessly, and fixed upon her his small, glittering eyes. The helper-out was embarrassedly moving kippers, tea and winkle-cache here and there to avoid getting in the ladies' and gentlemen's way.

'Why doan't yon chap wi't' beard git oop an' stop yon guzzlin' chap?' muttered Reuben, peering at the scene from behind the kitchen window-curtain, 'oopsettin' t' poor heathen an' yon meeky chap fra' Lunnon – 'tes a black shame, an' if I had not mislaid me goat-pistol –'

'Do ee come an' hev ee's tea, lovey,' pleaded Nancy from the table.

'Leave me a-be, Nancy Dolour. 'Tes dark days at Cold Comfort, look ee, wi' th' old place cockered up like a teg on Farish's Eve an' th' Pussy's Dinner runnin' hail an' farewell over all th' brashy land, an' me – an' *me*, as used t' *own* th' old place, wi' nought to till but a piece no bigger nor th' sheets on our bridal bed –'

'Shame on ee, afore th' liddle souls!'

''Twill do 'em no harm, eh, bodies all?' and Reuben glanced at the indifferent and treacle-bedaubed countenances of his offspring. 'It fair cappurtzes me to see th' old place overrun wi' such cattle (nay, 'tes an insult to th' honest beasts so to call 'em) as *they*,' jerking his head towards the delegates.

'Ay, 'tes sad enough. But Reuben, lovey,' Nancy went on, timidly yet with resolution, 'will ee not write a letter to all our chaps askin' 'em to come whoam agen? Nen ee could all work t' farm agen, like when I were a liddle maid.'

Reuben's face purpled and he crashed his fist upon his open palm.

'Niver! niver! niver! I ha' swore, and I mun keep me oath, ay, though th' farm be turned into a – a – tea-gardens, or a air-port wi' wickud gurt airyplanes all over ut. *I mun Till th' land Wi th' lone hand*, for though there be no longer Starkadders at Cold Comfort, there still be one at Ticklepenny's Field. Now eat up, bodies all' (an unnecessary instruction, since the children had never once stopped eating), 'an' let's hear no more o' letters ter foreign parts. What wull be, wull be,' and he sat down at the table and put half the loaf into his mouth.

Nancy said no more. She busied herself with waiting upon her family, but when the opportunity occurred she stealthily tied a knot in her apron-string. It would remind her to consult, as soon as she could find her alone, with Mrs Fairford.

6

On the next day, which was Tuesday, the one-day Exhibition of Transitorist Art was to be held, and throughout the morning Maser Messe slaved in a fury of creation behind locked doors, staggering out covered with dough, dye and sausage-meat at one o'clock in good time for luncheon. The rest of the delegates attended a lecture, on *Angst: Its Causes and Cultivation*, given by the Swedish Existentialist Greetë Grümbl (lovely fair hair and dark eyes – all wasted). Flora, glancing in at the audience while passing the Greate Kitchene window, saw them all busily scribbling notes except Mr Claud Hubris, who was scribbling a cheque for a diamond bracelet.

She was about to re-read letters from home which had arrived that morning and which pressure of work had until now prevented her from fully digesting, and the continuing fine weather tempted her to sit while doing so in one of the many small gardens.

As she passed the Greate Barne she heard a noise as of dismal weeping.

Oh blow! thought Flora, and was turning off smartly in the opposite direction when the voice of duty sounded in her ear. Sighing, she turned round, and went towards the Greate Barne.

The dim light and smell of ancient dirty straw which had formerly impressed the observer as characteristic of the Greate Barne had been banished with the Greate Barne's cobwebs and dusty walls, and it now glared with a patent white distemper and was illuminated at night by imitation candles in wrought-iron sconces with false wax dribbling down them. Flora was pleased to notice, however, that some swallows were already making their usual mess up in the roof.

This was the first time that she had entered the Greate Barne, and thus she had not before seen the wooden cubicles constructed by the Trust along its west wall to house the Starkadder maidens. They were alternately painted pink, blue and mauve, and each had a door-knocker made like a Cornish pixie.

The remainder of the Greate Barne's wall and floor space was occupied by pictures (at least, by things surrounded with frames) and some very large objects made of stone, wood and wire. A notice above an empty table evidently awaiting Messe's works read: *Exhibition of Transitorist Art. Here to-day, Gone, alas, this evening. Grab 'Em Pronto!*

The sound of weeping came from behind the cubicle doors. Flora approached a mauve one and knocked upon it.

There was the usual apprehensive Starkadder silence. Then a female voice wailed:

'Poor souls! Poor souls! Leave us weep i' peace!'

Flora opened the door and looked in.

Prone upon the pallet, with her skirt flung over her head, lay a form which Flora recognized, by the structure of its corset-cover, as Letty Starkadder, for she herself had in fact supplied the pattern for this identical garment sixteen years ago from the *Jardin des Modes*, and Letty had adapted it to her own rather peculiar shape.

'Letty!' said Flora, kindly but firmly. 'What is the matter? Has Caraway –?'

For Letty, known among the Starkadders as Our Caraway's Bespoke, had been betrothed to him for twenty-two years.

'Nay, Miss Poste. Caraway eats hearty an' du write me ivvery Lammas-tide,' answered Letty, in muffled tones from under her skirt.

'What is it, then? You are all crying; I can hear you.'

Howls and wails were indeed issuing from the other cubicles.

'Do sit up and re-arrange yourself,' Flora continued more severely. 'You would not like one of the gentlemen visitors to see you so.'

Letty howled so loudly at the words 'gentlemen visitors' that Flora's apprehensions became grave indeed, but she sat up and adjusted her skirt, though sobbing all the time.

'Now, what is it all about?' asked Flora, advancing into the tiny cell crowded with texts and quaking-grass and a huge coloured photograph of Caraway in the costume of a *voortrekker*.

''Tes they things out there!' exclaimed Letty fearfully, pointing through the open door. 'Two gurt men did bring 'em in while us was eatin' our nuncheon, a fat chap i' velvet trowses an' a grey chap like a corpse from' Lunnon.'

Mr Mybug and Hacke, thought Flora.

'And the – er – pictures and statues frightened all of

you? I can quite understand that. But they are only paint and wood and wire, you know; they cannot hurt you unless they actually fall on the top of you,' she said.

'Us knows that, Miss Poste. 'Tesn't that, Miss Poste. 'Tes th' poor souls as *made* 'em as we be weepin' for, not for fear o' they things. Fancy *wantin'* to make sich things, Miss Poste! Poor souls, poor souls!' and off she went again.

'An' 'tes puttin' us off of our arter-dinner cuppa,' observed a sombre voice at the door, where Jane Starkadder now appeared; 'for us ha'unt th' heart to drink, for pity, an' what's more, t' milk ha' turned mooky.'

The pale, timid faces of the other Starkadder maidens, swollen with weeping, now appeared one by one behind Jane's large, pasty countenance as they crept forth from their cells, and they all gazed lugubriously at Flora, giving her a sensation as if she were surrounded by a flock of sheep.

'Now stop crying, all of you,' she commanded briskly, 'and I will tell you what to do.'

But they only continued to stare dolefully, and Phoebe suddenly burst into fresh sobs:

'Yon things must ha' taken weeks to fashion! Th' poor souls as made 'em must ha' had to look at 'em all that long time! Fair breaks me heart to think o't!'

'Then do not think of it, please. Now have you any large, clean tea-cloths?' asked Flora.

They all nodded.

'Plenty o' they, gurt strong uns, us has got.'

'Us don't go fer to use un fer wipin' our platters much, Miss Poste.'

'Nay, for 'tes little us eats since th' chaps went to South Afriky.'

'Then go and fetch the largest tea-cloths you have, and hang them over the – er – those things out there. Then you won't see them, will you?'

A murmur of relief arose:

'Ay, 'tes true, surelie.'

''Tes a likely notion, Miss Poste.'

'Good. Then, after you have drunk a strong cup of tea (I have a tin of milk, which Prue may fetch from my bedroom), you can go down to the church and say a prayer for the gentlemen who made those – er – the things. That will make a peaceful little excursion for you,' concluded Flora.

The countenances of the maidens brightened, and they nodded almost eagerly, while they began to straighten their bodices and bootlaces and to tweak and pat their hair.

'Ay, that wull be th' thing tu du,' murmured Susan, 'for th' poor souls as made them monster things must be in hell-fire, surelie.'

Flora thought that it would use up valuable energy and be boring to herself if she attempted to explain to Susan that, far from being generally regarded as dwellers in hell-fire, Hacke, Messe and Peccavi were revered by their contemporaries as New Masters and great artists; gifted spirits who, unlike some of the Old Masters, made large sums from selling their works to the thirsting herd.

Smilingly declining the slab of grey cake proffered her by Hetty, she strolled out into the Greate Barne, seated herself upon a lump of oddly-shaped stone at the foot of *Woman with Wind* (or it may have been *Woman with Child*; she had difficulty in remembering which was which) and began to peruse her letters. She thought it as well to remain near at hand, in case the female Starkadders should again need her help, for no one else ever helped them, so far as she could make out, and they seemed to her to have a pretty thin time.

Having finished reading her letters and reflected with satisfaction that all went well at the Vicarage, she put them away in her pocket and surveyed the now animated scene in the Greate Barne, which already suggested, rather than an exhibition of modern art, airing day at the Snow-White Laundry. She had completely forgotten that the Exhibition of Transitorist Art was to open at half-past two; and while she was interestedly watching the attempts of Prue and Jane to stretch an extra large tea-cloth across the front of *Woman with Child* (or it may have been *Woman with Wind*), and reflecting that their task was made no easier by the fact that both kept their eyes modestly averted, a voice cried angrily:

'What goes on here?'

Flora turned round. There stood Hacke, Mr Mybug, Peccavi in an immaculate grey suit, Riska in black petticoats and mantilla with two bones in her hair (quite a piece of Old Portugal this afternoon, thought Flora) and Messe laden with a trayful of statuettes made from pastry and sausage-meat and coloured with pea-green and ox-blood dyes.

'Good heavens! Flora, don't sit on that! It's my Found Object!' cried Mr Mybug, pointing dramatically at the lump of oddly-shaped stone. 'I'd no time to create anything fresh for this show.'

'Vhat means it all?' screamed Hacke, rushing across to *Woman with Wind* (or the other one) and snatching down the tea-cloth, 'Hidink my vork avay! Und der Peccavi-artvorke also! Sabotage!'

'Not at all,' retorted Flora. 'Delicate objects must be protected from dust and glare,' and, wishing to prevent more fuss, she got up (with some relief) from Found Object, which Mr Mybug at once rolled two inches farther away from her, surveying it with his head on one side to see if she had damaged its rude contours.

Her explanation was only partly accepted.

'In Inklandt no such trouble is done for der art-verks,' snapped Messe. 'Der Inklish no artists or art-verks of der own haf, und so dey jealous are off der Masters off der Europe.'

Here two coughs sounded one after another in the background from two professors of Genetics, Breed and Brood, who were the first visitors to the Exhibition, and Messe hurried off to arrange the first tray-load of statuettes (for Flora observed with dismay that a second and third were being carried in by two Managerial Revolutionaries) upon the shelves. Hacke took the two Professors to see Peccavi's *The Excreta*, snatching off tea-cloths in passing as he went, and Riska and Peccavi squatted on the floor and played some Portuguese game with the bones from Riska's hair. Every now and again they shouted 'Holá!' and kicked out at each other's shins.

'He's entered upon a new phase,' muttered Mr Mybug to Flora, jerking his head towards Peccavi. 'He's younger, gayer, less remote in his approach.'

'Is he?'

'It's *her*. She's responsible for his new gaiety.'

'Holá!' shouted Riska, catching Peccavi a crack on the shin that rang through the Greate Barne.

'He's begun a new series of works,' continued Mr Mybug, 'light, gay, irresistible forms leaping and playing. Oh, superb.'

'They sound charming,' said Flora, knowing full well that no matter what they sounded like, they would look simply awful.

'Such primitive joy!'

'Is he feeling better? I am glad.'

Anybody who had seen Peccavi's last exhibition, she thought, couldn't help being glad.

'When will they be shown?' she went on, 'I must keep a look out for them.'

'Oh, he won't show them in *England*. *We* shan't see them. (I'm privileged; I've been allowed one Glimpse because Tom Jones and I are doing something on them for "Nadir".) But please don't suppose, my dear Flora, that *we* shall have the first sight of these magnificent things. What have *we* done to deserve them?'

What, indeed, thought Flora. Besides, we haven't the money to buy them with.

'Then where will they be shown?' she asked.

'New York. And that is *not* only because America is now the richest country. It's because New York is now what Paris once was: Art Centre of the world. *He* isn't like that, you know. He doesn't care for money. Give him a pool and some paint, and Piccolo Peccavi can breathe.'

Peccavi and Riska, bored with the bones game, were now engaged in alternately pulling one another's ears and noses.

'Primitive games. I've seen the Portuguese gipsies do

81

that,' commented Mr Mybug, watching them with some complacence.

Flora also had cause for complacence, for out of the corner of her eye she detected a procession of female Starkadders, in outdoor attire and carrying prayer-books, wending its way unobtrusively along the far end of the Greate Barne towards the other door.

Shortly afterwards she made her excuses to Mr Mybug and left him to the pleasures of the Exhibition, which were now in full swing.

That evening, after supervising the delegates' after-dinner coffee-swigging (a harsh word, but Mr Jones and Professor Farine were never content with less than six cups apiece and most of the delegates took three), Flora wrapped herself in her old cloak of viridian-green velvet and walked across the uplands to Haute-Couture Hall, where she found that all the sons and daughters had been allowed to stay up to meet her. In reminiscences and laughter, in mutual discoveries and in the relating of family news and the laying of plans for future meetings, two hours passed in one delightful flash, and it was after eleven o'clock when, having said good-night to Hereward, who had accompanied her with a posse of dogs as far as the summit of Teazeaunt Beacon, Flora began the walk down to Cold Comfort Farm.

It was a clear, moonlit night, but she had just entered the dense shade cast by the thicket of flowering elder-trees growing beside the stile, when a figure with a scarf tied about its head stepped forward in the scented gloom and a female voice said timidly:

'Be ut Mis' Fairford? Could I have a word wi' ee?'

Flora was naturally startled, for her thoughts at that

moment had been busy with Judith Starkadder, who, Elfine had informed her, had entered a rather peculiar Sisterhood, spiritually guided by one Père Hyacinthe, in a fashionable Riviera town. However, she answered, 'Certainly, Nancy,' in a cheerful enough tone, though with sinking heart.

Fortunately Nancy had not completely imbibed the Starkadder technique of prolonging any agony that might be on tap, and she got off the mark pretty fast.

'Oh, Mis' Fairford!' she sighed, clasping her hands as they walked on together, ''tes Reuben, my man! Un's heart is fair breakin' to see th' farm in thiccy state, but un will not write to all th' chaps asking 'em to come whoam agen.'

'What good could they do if they did come, Nancy? It would probably only make things worse.'

'Nay, they could work th' farm agen, Mis' Fairford. Lookee, th' gennelman as did come fro' Lunnon did say as if our Reuben could find seven good men an' true, th' old place could earn its keep agen. (Ay, he were a nice-spoken gennelman. He did gie our Nan a lot o' they paper-forms for to make dollses bedden-cloes, but our Reuben he couldn't abide he.)'

'It is that tiresome Oath, I suppose, that is keeping Reuben from writing to them?' said Flora thoughtfully.

'Ay, Mis' Fairford.'

'Do you happen to know who he swore it to?'

'Nay, niver ask me that, Mis' Fairford,' answered Nancy fearfully, with a touch of Starkadder.

'Why on earth shouldn't I ask you, Nancy? I am as anxious as you are to see the Farm at work again. Do be sensible.'

They had paused near the garden of Reuben's cottage,

and by the light of the moon they could clearly see the farm in the hollow. All was peaceful and silent except for a slight commotion taking place on the cottage back-doorstep, where the Sage had detected the follower in laying a pinch of tea-leaves before a small idol which he had concealed in his loin cloth. It had six arms and an elephant's head, and the Sage was gently rebuking him. The follower was bawling softly and beating his breast, and the helper-out, much disturbed, was shaking his head, sucking his pipe and making up the fire, all as quietly as possible, for fear of awakening the household within doors.

''Tes because I doan't know to who Reuben did be-swear th' Oath that I says "Doan't ask me," Mis' Fairford,' Nancy said mildly at length.

'Then why couldn't you simply say "I don't know", Nancy? You really must try not to get into Starkadder ways, you know, especially now you have all those children to bring up. Whatever would happen if you tried mending their clothes and cooking their food Starkadder-fashion?'

'But I be a Starkadder, Mis' Fairford — by wedlock, leastways. Reuben do say so. An' come to that, us Dolours bean't much,' ended Nancy on a resigned note.

'Nonsense. I remember your father, Mark Dolour, as — er — a fine, upstanding man; not very cheerful, perhaps, but who would be after working for years for the Starkadders? However, never mind him now. Have you any idea at all who Reuben *might* have sworn the Oath to?'

'Nay, Mis' Fairford. Our Reuben be a close 'un when he du like.'

'You have never asked him?'

'Niver, Mis' Fairford; no, niver. I du fear to speak o' it.'

'But you *must*, Nancy, if you want the Starkadders to come home and the farm to get to work again. Now you must ask him who he swore it to tomorrow, at dinner-time, and come in the evening to tell me what he says. Will you do that?'

'Ay, I wull try, Mis' Fairford,' Nancy answered, with reviving cheerfulness, 'an' I du take it most kind o' ee to bear such pains fer me an' mine.'

Flora replied kindly that the welfare of Cold Comfort Farm and the Starkadders had always been of interest to her, surprise at Nancy's pretty manners adding warmth to her tones, and so they bade one another good night. Flora went upstairs to her attic bedchamber well pleased with the evening's events, for a workable plan had now taken shape in her head, and she soon fell asleep, but in more than one room at the farm wakeful souls were wrestling in unnecessary anguish or sitting up frightening themselves with a large and boring book.

7

Wednesday was to be occupied by a Reading Party. The delegates were to drive through a stretch of breezy, open country to a wooded valley, where they would partake of luncheon, and afterwards each one would read aloud from some vital volume dealing with an important coeval activity. Flora was to accompany the party to supervise the serving of luncheon. (No one had suggested that *she* should read anything aloud; she owed this escape to Mr Mybug's low opinion of her taste in books, for although he had muttered something about 'getting Flora Fairford to read something – why shouldn't she – do her good, she's always Dodging Reality', he had immediately afterwards shaken his head and decided that it would only be a waste of precious time to listen to the sort of twaddle Flora would be likely to choose. Besides, he wanted to secure as much time as possible for his own reading from *The Dromedary*, the beastly little work before referred to.)

At the appointed time the delegates assembled in the Greate Yarde, where a brake drawn by two horses waited to convey them to the chosen valley. Everyone seemed satisfied with the method of conveyance except Frau Dichtverworren, who admitted with a bass laugh that she had a fixation on fast cars, adoring to rush through the burning summer air until all sense of time, place, personality and public safety had vanished; and Peccavi. *He* of course, had discovered an old bicycle among some junk in a shed. It had a trailer, and he and Riska proposed riding it in turns, and Riska wore shorts with a hole in and a very tight jumper in anticipation of this feat. Mr Mybug pointed out to Flora how enviously the other delegates watched their gay, childish absorption in their new toy. Flora herself was to ride in a converted jeep with the luncheon baskets, a portable steel bar, and the drink.

Mr Jones was grumbling that there would be flies in the woods and no champagne.

'Yes, there will, a magnum of it. The President of the French Republic sent it over this morning. That was the aeroplane we heard about six o'clock,' said Flora to him, as she and the helper-out staggered across the yard with a hamper of delicacies.

'Ah! *La belle France! Magnifique!*' cried Mr Jones, and kissed his fingers to Mdlle Avaler, who now sauntered up smiling, with Ruggieiro on *Existentialism* under one arm and the new number of *Chiffons* under the other.

Flora and the helper-out were half-way across the yard with the second hamper when the helper-out, moistening his lips, said hoarsely:

'Beggin' your pardon, mum. The gentleman.'

'I know whom you mean. What about him?' said Flora encouragingly. There could be only one person at the Conference thus identified in the minds of both the helper-out and herself, and that was the Sage, though he did have no clothes and apparently no bank balance.

''E was a-wishin' 'e could go on the picnic, mum. I 'ears
'im. Then 'is friend tells me as 'ow 'e wouldn't *ask* to come,
cos with 'im, if you take my meanin', mum, it's always Self-
Denial Week. But 'e would *like* to go, mum. I do know that.'

'I will see what can be done,' replied Flora, glancing at
the watch upon her bosom and feeling that the Sage's
patriarchal beauty and serenity might cheer up the proceedings a bit, especially if there were to be a long reading
from *The Dromedary*.

She found the Sage meditating by the fire. The follower,
looking subdued and mournful, was washing his master's
robe in Nancy's tub.

'Peace,' said the Sage as she approached.

'And to you also, Teacher. I say, I've been thinking – it's
a fine day, and it would make a change for you –'

'All change is evil, daughter, even as are all aimless
hurryings from babob tree to cabob tree, and all cranings
over railings to gape at monkeys or parrots.'

'How exhausting you make it sound!' smiled Flora. 'But
you will not have to hurry or crane over railings, because
there is a carriage to take you to the picnic –'

'The very name is full of distractions. In this one's own
land it is called "fool's food".'

'No doubt, but I do wish you would go, Teacher. Will
you not tell your ignorant daughter of the west,' coaxed
Flora, kneeling beside him, 'why you will not go?'

'I desire to go, daughter. I desire to see again the Black
Water and the unfamiliar trees, for in youth, this one was
a painter of such illusory things upon wood and silk. All
desire leads to attachment, and all attachment is evil.
Therefore, I must let my desire die, and I must not go.'

Flora gazed at him in perplexity. His superb mild eyes were cast downwards in thought, and only the gasps of the follower slowly forcing folds of wet cotton through Nancy's wringer broke the morning stillness. Then Flora smiled.

'If you were carried to the carriage by force, Teacher, would you attempt to resist?' she asked.

'No, daughter. All resistance to force is evil.'

'Good!' said Flora, and hastened away to find two strong men.

Of course no one wanted the task, and indeed most of the delegates were in such a state from non-stop drinking, chain smoking, sleepless nights, strong coffee and complexes that they would not have been able even had they been willing; but Flora persuaded Mr Jones and one of the Managerial Revolutionaries who had specialized in the Theory and Practice of Weight-Lifting to carry the Sage to the brake.

I can understand people being afraid of these Revolutionaries, thought Flora, sailing triumphantly in the wake of the Sage borne in a bandy chair between Mr Jones and the weight-lifting expert, but they are useful. One of them stuck new rubbers on my shoes last night, and this morning another got the screw-top off that bottle in *no* time. Of course, the first one can *only* stick rubbers on shoes, and the other hasn't a clue to *anything* except getting screw-tops off bottles, and it does give them a *fearful* power over people who aren't specialists, but say what you like, they *are* useful.

'Bear witness, daughter, that I was borne here by force and did not resist,' said the Sage, as his bearers bumped him down in the seat next to the driver of the brake.

'Of course, Teacher. Oh' – suddenly recollecting – 'how about your follower? Can he come, too?'

'He has sinned, daughter,' said the Sage mildly.

'I know. Last night; I saw him. But it's such a nice day and –'

'His spiritual eyes are darkened and he lusteth· after images of the unimaginable.'

'He will learn better, surely, Teacher?'

'In time, daughter, and if not there, in Eternity. But his feet are hardly yet set upon the Path.'

'I'm sure he wants to go to the picnic, Teacher.'

'Doubtless, daughter. He lusteth also after distractions. Even now, doubtless, he weeps.'

'I'll go and get him,' said Flora decidedly, and hastened away, for the delegates were beginning to climb into the brake and squabble over who should sit where and with whom.

She found the follower weeping hopelessly into the washtub, while the Sage's clean yellowish-pink robe flapped on the line above his head.

'Cheer up!' said Flora, feeling she ought to step out of a pumpkin and wave a wand. 'You're going to the picnic. Yes, he says you can. Hurry up and put on a clean wreath or something' (for the follower usually wore a lopsided circle of the commonest weeds on his head), 'you haven't too much time.'

The follower rushed into a bush, reappearing almost immediately with his cooking-pot in one hand, while with the other he tried to adjust a rough-dried loincloth round his waist and a ceremonial wreath of sukebind upon his head. Flora raised her eyebrows at the sukebind, which presumably he had chosen for its showy pink flowers, but there was no time to explain why she was rebuking him about it, even if she did; also, in her opinion he had been rebuked enough.

He gave one glance at the roof of a shed too high for him to reach, where presumably the Sage had bestowed his forbidden idol, then salaamed to Flora, and scurried away with an expression almost of eagerness upon his dim black face.

'No room for a little one,' observed a depressed voice behind her, and she turned and saw the helper-out. 'I'm not complainin',' he instantly added.

Flora having told him that he might accompany her in the converted jeep, they hurried off to take their places, and found the follower already coiled amidst the hampers.

The party was now ready to start, but was delayed for a few moments longer by Mr Mybug, who had lingered to peruse a boring letter from Rennett about repairs to the kitchen ceiling ('How can I be expected to have energy for My Own Stuff when I am continually hounded by these details?' demanded Mr Mybug of Mr Jones, who was not listening), and who rushed up with his garments (contributed by the American *Darn it – And Clothe Britain* Guild) in some disarray. However, at last the cavalcade set off; headed by the brake, followed by Mrs Ernestine Thump in her little car driven by the depressed girl chauffeur, and with its rear brought up by Flora in the converted jeep. The latter was driven by an oiled youth from Howling village who had been pointed out to her as a cadet of the Dolour family, by name Hick. He drove with assured recklessness, and his manner was so aloof that she was pleased to use it as an excuse not to address him.

Of Peccavi and Riska there was no sign.

The brake kept just ahead of the jeep, and pretty soon Flora could detect that all was not well with its occupants. Arms were waving, faces empurpled, and even fragments of sentences floated down to her – 'Heidigger' – 'angst' – 'l'homme est ce qu'il faut' – 'wahl' – 'the Common man' – 'the id' – and streams of unintelligible symbols shouted by the physicists, some of whom were hanging helplessly over the side of the brake, overcome by that sense of the unreality of all perceived phenomena (and even of the visual sense enabling them to be perceived, if perceived they were) which frequently caused them to have hysterical fits. Mr Mybug, Mr Jones and Mdlle Avaler appeared to be arguing with Mr Hubris and Frau Dichtverworren, with Messe and Hacke nipping in with a nasty crack whenever they understood enough of what was being said to get one home.

The Sage had apparently gone off into a trance (I can't blame him, thought Flora, but it is a pity that he is missing this charming scenery).

The vehicles were now ascending a steep chalk road, and suddenly she became aware of a moth-like fluttering on her foot. She glanced downwards, and saw black fingers just withdrawing from her shoelace, and, turning her gaze upon the follower, she was barely in time to detect him withdrawing his beady eyes from her face before he turned his head with a snake-like movement towards the dip in the downs where had suddenly appeared the sea. At the same time he salaamed towards the glittering mass, and it was plain that he had wanted to draw her attention to it.

'Very fine, very good,' smiled and nodded Flora.

'Lovely smell o' kippers,' muttered the helper-out, removing his bowler hat and shutting his eyes.

Reflecting that the appreciative spirit of her companions more than compensated for their lack of conversation, Flora devoted herself to preventing the hampers from sliding out of the jeep, which now began to descend into a narrow valley filled with woods. On the way they passed Peccavi and Riska, smacking at one another amid the ruins of the trailer and bicycle. Riska had a black eye, which might be due either to the accident or to Peccavi, and although the occupants of the brake looked at them with awed envy, no one suggested that they should be given a lift.

In a moment the vehicles entered a wood of beeches thickened to almost tropical density and lustre of leaf by the moist valley air. Under such thick canopies there could be no grassy glades suitable for picnicking, and the dark leafy soil was damp, but along either edge of the road ran low banks riddled with warrens and covered in moss, and when the brake reached a spot where sunlight burst through thinner branches the driver (after fruitlessly suggesting to its furiously-arguing occupants that 'Ere Was A Nice Place) pulled up, and climbed down from his seat. Mrs Ernestine Thump at once dug her finger into the depressed girl driver's neck, at the same time bawling at her down a speaking-tube, and Hick Dolour stopped the jeep and climbed out.

'Fag?' he enquired amiably of Flora, taking two from behind his ear.

Flora unsmilingly but courteously declined.

'Suits me,' said Hick Dolour, and retired behind the mossy bank and went to sleep.

The delegates were now alighting from the brake, still arguing, and Mrs Ernestine Thump rushed up to them and plunged in with a joyous splash, while Flora, the follower and the helper-out unloaded the hampers from the jeep and began to assemble the portable bar.

'When do we "feed"?' demanded Mr Mybug, bustling up with his bosom unbuttoned and disagreeably exposed on account of the heat. 'I say, you ought to have been with us, Flora! Hacke was in superb form – coruscatingly malicious – God, that man has a tongue like a viper! And Messe is the perfect foil to him – slow, heavy, brutally impenetrable. It was a verbal beating-up; the best thing I've heard in years.'

'It does sound fun. Do you think you could help unpack the sandwiches? It takes three people to assemble this bar, and the delegates are looking hungry.'

'My dear girl, I'd love to, but as a matter of fact I promised Ernie Thump I'd keep a look out at the cross-roads for Bob Flatte. He's going to give us themes from *The Flayed* on a recorder, you know, and Ernie's afraid he'll miss the way.'

Flora suppressed the retort that Mrs Ernestine Thump's fears had (musically, at any rate) long ago been realized, and waved Mr Mybug off with a pleasant smile, for she had observed the depressed girl chauffeur lingering near at hand, and deduced that she was about to offer her services. Mr Mybug bounded joyously away, and the depressed girl chauffeur drew near and muttered:

'Shall I muck in –'ow about it, I meantersay?'

Flora accepted the offer with gratitude, and soon they had the bar assembled, the drinks and glasses arranged, and Mr Jones installed behind it as barman, he having jeeringly waved aside a Managerial Revolutionary, who had written a thesis on *The Psychology of the Alcoholic Norm* and taken a six-months' course in Alcoholic Dispensemanship, and timidly offered to help. The sandwiches, patties and pies were then unpacked, and, the cloth having been spread upon a comparatively flat expanse of mossy ground and the collation arranged thereon, the party seated itself in a large circle, and Mr Claud Hubris uncorked the first bottle of champagne, whose cork flew so high that it vanished glittering among the leaves of the beech boughs overhead.

Flora had caused to be arranged a smaller cloth for herself and her companions at a distance from the main party, retired enough to be agreeable, but not so obviously withdrawn as to invite comment. Only Mdlle Avaler, on her way to the seat of honour beside Mr Hubris, paused to inspect their modest preparations (drawn, no doubt, by that curiosity on the part of intellectuals about the domestic arrangements of unintellectuals to which reference has already been made).

'How cool an' *confortable* you arre! Shell I come an' sit weez you?'

'The gentlemen could not spare you,' smilingly replied Flora, hoping that the look of extreme terror which had appeared upon the countenances of the follower and the helper-out at Mdlle Avaler's suggestion would not be observed by the young lady herself.

However, the latter only screwed up her great sea-coloured eyes in a naughty smile and sauntered away to sit with Mr Hubris, and in a moment Flora and her companions felt sufficiently at their ease to begin upon the patties, Flora having already invited the depressed girl chauffeur to share their repast.

The larger party had not long been settled at their eating, drinking, and arguing before Peccavi and Riska came bumping down the forest path, crying with shrieks of laughter that they had stolen two bicycles belonging to a priest and a nurse-person who had stupidly left them outside a church. They did not dismount at the edge of the group, but rode right across the table-cloth into the midst of the brilliant throng, Riska overbalancing on top of Professor Farine, who snatched her to him with a delighted roar and Peccavi being brought to earth by a bowl of orange jelly which deflected his front wheel. Their appetites and spirits were unaffected by this incident; Peccavi, indeed, was in top-hole form, accusing the ladies of all the most refined vices in a shout with his mouth full and pointing at them with a black, painty finger. When he paused for breath, W. W. R. Token took over, relating stories told him off the record by his psychiatrist. The fun was beginning to be rather fast and the scientists were already furious, while lobster patties, caviar toast, and cucumber sandwiches vanished in enormous quantities, and at the bar Mr Jones was kept busy dishing out absinthe and champagne.

Suddenly a shout drew attention to Mr Mybug, who was seen coming down the path accompanied by a tall bald man irreproachably dressed in grey, who carried a recorder, and looked very, very sad. Bob Flatte, the composer, had arrived to carry out his threat. Behind him staggered his secretary, bearing two suitcases containing the score of *The Flayed*.

Flatte announced his intention of blowing the themes at once, as he had to return immediately to town for a rehearsal of his new work, and Flora had barely time to pass to her companions the ear-plugs which she had thoughtfully provided, before the secretary had hauled the score out of the suitcases, Flatte had fluttered through the first four hundred pages of it with a speed resulting from weeks of practice, found the place where the Weeping Skeleton theme enters, leant against a tree, and began to blow.

For some fifteen minutes Flora and her party placidly ate their luncheon in a perfect silence, Flora occasionally glancing across at the brilliant throng, where Flatte was blowing away like mad and everybody looked absolutely miserable.

For the benefit of readers who are not familiar with the work of Flatte it may be remarked that *The Flayed* is typical of his latest and most powerful manner, and deals with the tragedy of two types named Stan Brusk and Em Wallow, living in a Bedfordshire village. Em is Stan's girl, but he loses her to Bert Scarr when the latter comes to work in the local tanning factory. Stan Brusk is a sadist who derives pleasure from tanning hides and has twice been publicly reproved by the foreman for gloating while at work. In a powerful recitative and aria Stan defies the foreman, describes the pleasures of tanning, and at last falls down exhausted under a vat.

A series of sinuous themes follows, intended to represent the smells from the vat winding over his unconscious body. In the dinner-hour Em creeps in with a pie, which she does not know has been poisoned by the fumes from the vat.

Bert Scarr then enters. He and Em sing a duet, in which Bert confesses that he has always had a secret craving to be flayed like one of the hides in the factory and Em expresses her horror and scorn of him. At last she falls under the vat on top of Stan, who recovers consciousness and misunderstands her action. Em, Stan and Bert are then overcome by fumes from the vat, and dream they are in Hell.

The Weeping Skeleton's song which follows has been said to refute, once and for all, the accusation that Flatte's operas lack light relief. The song may not express humour as it is generally understood, but to deny that the theme of four minor chords given out in *glissando* form by the first violin and repeated in fugue form by solo instruments one after the other until it ends abruptly on the drums is expressive of a rationalized and resigned humour (perhaps most akin to irony) is merely imperceptive.

Em recovers first and revives Bert with a piece of the pie. The foreman comes in accompanied by a chorus of Operatives and Tanners and accuses Bert of slacking. Bert, already poisoned, and driven by his neurosis, jumps into the vatful of skins and is suffocated. Em eats some pie and dies. Stan stabs the foreman with his penknife (a present from his mother on his seventh birthday and symbolizing her neurotic hold over him) and the foreman dies. While Stan is singing the Flagellation Song and driving out the chorus of Operatives and Tanners with a whip, his mother, Widow Brusk, enters. After she has sung an aria in which she confesses that Stan is the illegitimate son of a taxidermist who seduced her in early youth, thus accounting for her son's sadistic obsession, Stan symbolically attempts to skin her and they both become insane. The opera then ends. It was to represent English music at the International Music Festival in the following year.

At length signs of restored animation upon the countenances of the audience and their gestures of admiration and gratitude, combined with Flatte's offhand nod, informed Flora that the treat was over, and she collected the earplugs (the follower attempted to keep his, but was gently dissuaded) and replaced them in her handbag.

'Please could I 'ave another sangwidge?' suddenly asked the depressed girl chauffeur. It was the first time that she had spoken above a murmur.

'Pray do,' and Flora handed her the cucumber ones.

'Thanks – thenks ever so, I meantersay.'

'No doubt Mrs Thump is so much occupied that you have few opportunities for regular meals?' pursued Flora, with sympathy.

'"Tain't that, so much, but she believes in fasting. She says it keeps the mind alert.'

'Indeed. Do you live at Mrs Thump's house?'

'I do since the family gave up the Chester Square house. I say,' and the chauffeur giggled as she waved her glass, 'I do like this – this here champagne. It's delicious – smeshin', I meantersay. I've often heard Daddy talk about it. Could I *possibly* have a spot more?'

'Of course.' Flora replenished her glass from the three bottles supplied for her party by Mr Jones. 'Is this the first time you have tasted champagne?'

'Yes. Daddy – Dad, meantersay, he couldn't never afford it, see,' and she drained her glass.

'A misfortune indeed. Is he – er – unemployed at the moment?'

'Well, he is rather. He's the Earl of Brackenbourne, as a matter of fact,' confessed the chauffeur, leaning towards Flora and earnestly wagging one finger, 'and I'm Lady Geraldine Tresswillian. Don't you love my little W.C. accent? I had two terms at RADA learning to say "eow", only when I'm tired or I've had one over the eight it slips up, see? Mustn't let Ma'am hear, must we?' she added confidentially, glancing towards Mrs Ernestine Thump. 'I have to call her Ma'am and she calls me Willian. Everybody thinks it's William, and that sounds queer. But it can't be helped,' she ended, smiling round upon them and holding out her glass for more champagne.

'I knew that thou wert of the Brahmin caste as soon as thou didst speak, daughter,' suddenly said the Sage, who had emerged some moments ago from a nearby glade where he had been engaged in meditation and seated himself cross-legged upon the fringe of Flora's party. 'Thy words were those of the Sweepers, but thy voice is soft as the night wind in the pine trees of the Hills.'

'Sweet,' answered Lady Geraldine, beaming upon him.

'Wot's it like, workin' for '*er*, gel?' hoarsely enquired the helper-out.

'Perfectly bloody, of course, but of course I'm frightfully lucky to have the job at all. I mean, with my normal accent and *no* typing or shorthand or economics or Commercial Spanish, and only a year in France and Uncle Augustine to teach me Greek (he's Master of Saint Osyth's), I mean I was *marvellously* lucky even to get an *interview*. And it *is* three pounds a week and occasional meals. I say, *do* you mind most awfully if I go to sleep?'

She extended herself upon the ground and shut her

eyes, and Flora removed her peaked cap and motioned to the follower to waft a chestnut fan, which he had gathered, to and fro above her delicate plain young face, but unfortunately at that moment Mrs Ernestine Thump, catching sight of oriental countenances, came plunging over to shake hands with their owners and congratulate them on Pakistan, to the extreme terror of the follower (who took her for an incarnation of Kali Goddess of Vengeance) and to the complete indifference of the Sage, who had never heard of Pakistan.

Mrs Ernestine Thump then decided that she would pay one of her visits to Little Drinking, which happy constituency was frequently shaken to its core by such unheralded descents on the part of its Member ('Remember, if *I* Represent *you*, *you* Represent *me*, and we must *both* be on our best behaviour,' as Mrs Ernestine Thump would declare to her constituents with a threatening laugh). She therefore stumped away to her car, bawling to her chauffeur to accompany her, and bawling to Bob Flatte in passing an offer to drop him, his secretary and the score of *The Flayed* at the nearest railway station.

Lady Geraldine, after one wink at Flora, became the depressed girl chauffeur again and went across to Mrs Ernestine Thump's car, and the Sage and the follower retired into a glade to go through the elaborate purification ritual made necessary by the handshake from Mrs Ernestine Thump.

Luncheon now being over and digested and the afternoon well advanced, it was decided among the delegates to proceed with the readings from contemporary works and unpublished writings by members of the Conference, and then to drive homewards. Accordingly Mr Mybug, who had devoted tireless energy to bringing about this result, eagerly stood up to open the proceedings with a reading from *The Dromedary*.

The author was a Bessarabian who was (temporarily, his admirers trusted) in a Home. The book *apparently* dealt with one day only in the life of a perfectly ordinary Middle East dromedary, but by voraciously rummaging beneath its seemingly innocuous paragraphs, the International Thinkers had discovered that the Dromedary was really the Universe, and the contents of its three stomachs (raw, digested, and all ready) were the Past, the Present and the Future. The Arab who tended it was really Man. Ah, but who was the Chief Date, the incalculable and apparently sinister but sometimes apparently benevolent figure who, at every turn (and there were a good lot of turns), by-passed or flummoxed the Arab, Bhee? Combining as it did the emotions roused by a game of Hare and Hounds with those inspired by the crossword puzzle in *The Times*, *The Dromedary* would have been considered by the International Thinkers well worth (had such a low thought ever entered their heads) the ten-and-sixpence demanded by its publishers.

Lolling against a young beech whose personal appearance contrasted strongly with his own, Mr Mybug in a low intense voice began to read:

'Soon Bhee woke up in his bed and heard the lorn voice that to most men was no more than a dromedary's grunt – 'Who will swill out my den? My den is damp and Bhee is still drunk'. Love, love, the words said too to him, but, sad and dry as ever after his bout, he could only think that today he must call upon the Chief Date to see if his dog, or perhaps it was the dog of the Chief Date, had come home. He did not know his way to the tent that he had been told was the tent of the Chief Date, for the tent that he had seen last night did not look the same as the tent he saw today. There was a dog by the fire when he went in but the Chief Date did not look up from his work on the mosaic. Bhee did not know if it was the same dog, and when the Chief Date quickly took off his fez, Bhee saw he was a man he had not seen before, but he had a look of the Chief Date and might have been him without his fez. The mosaic looked as if it might be the same mosaic. Bhee sat down on the carpet and the dog made to bite him.'

This went on for nearly three-quarters of an hour, interrupted only by murmurs of 'Superb' and occasional sly chuckles of appreciation, and then, after Mr Mybug had done, and the feverish applause had ceased, Mdlle Avaler stood up looking positively edible in a cream muslin gown with bright grey ribbons and began to read a poem written in a mixture of English and German by an Existentialist Italian poet residing at Padua. Though it went like this:

> Swathed in nought the *Dasein* is,
> *Geworfen* like a shard;
> Values antithetical
> Of salve and sin
> Yield not to dialectical –
>   (and so forth)

Flora could not detect any signs of irritation or boredom upon the faces of the audience, and she decided that this was partly because some of them actually did understand what the poem meant (and much good *that* does them, she thought) and partly because the gentlemen, at least, enjoyed contemplating the cruel charms of Mdlle Avaler's twenty summers.

The proceedings continued with a reading by a Managerial Revolutionary from the pamphlet entitled *The Replacement of Electric Fuses in the Typical Fuse-Container*, this being chosen as representative of the contemporary technical literature on the subject. Someone then slavishly suggested that Mr Hubris be invited to read from a work entitled *The Managerial Function*, but as no one dared to go behind the tree where he lay with his cigars and a dirty book and wake him up, the idea was allowed to drop, and a dim scientist, doped with ether, read aloud two pages from a completely unintelligible work on atomic physics in an inaudible voice before he collapsed. He was briskly hauled aside by two of the Managerial Revolutionaries, and amid a murmur of relieved applause the proceedings came to an end.

'Have you had a good day, Teacher?' asked Flora, as the Sage strode past her on his way to the brake. It was plain to see that amidst the bustle of departure and the necessity of restraining the follower's desires, he had forgotten to await the two strong men who should carry him unresisting to his place, and Flora was relieved, for it meant that she would not have to fag round arranging it.

'No, daughter. Monkey has been present; Monkey has been running here and there scratching himself and sniffing out distractions and causing feet to stray from the Path.'

'Oh dear. Didn't you even like the fresh air and the cucumber sandwiches?'

'The food was a device of Monkey, daughter; I did not eat it. But contemplation' – glancing at the beech trees in the late afternoon light – 'permitted this one' – touching his breast – 'and that one' – glancing at the follower – 'to acquire a little, a very little, merit. The day has not been entirely given over to Monkey.'

He salaamed and went on his way, and the follower scurried after him. His expression was remorseful and glum, but this was only to be expected, for whenever Flora had happened to catch sight of him throughout the day he had appeared to be very much given over to Monkey.

The departure of the cortège was delayed for some surprising moments while the helper-out, who had been resting his naked what he called plates-of-meat on the moss, pantingly resumed socks and boots under the lofty and incredulous gaze of all the delegates (Mr Claud Hubris could hardly believe his eyes, and almost made a note of the affair with a view to lodging a complaint to the Organizing Secretary), but it set off at last, and the home-ward journey passed without untoward incident.

8

'Come in,' called Flora, in response to a soft tap upon the door of the Green Parlour, where she sat writing a letter to Charles after dinner on the evening of that same day.

Nancy entered, neatly dressed as always and looking pensive.

'Good evening, Nancy. Sit down, won't you?' said Flora briskly, putting aside her letter. 'Now how did you get on? Did you ask Reuben to whom he swore the Oath?'

'Oh yes, Mis' Fairford, arter tea.'

'And did he tell you?'

'Oh no, Mis' Fairford.'

'Was he annoyed?'

'Oh yes, Mis' Fairford. 'Twere goreish. Un did have a fit, like.'

'How tiresome. But he wouldn't tell you?'

'Un couldna. Un's face was beswole and un's eyes beblooded wi' rage an' un did foam –'

'Yes, it must have been very distressing. I hope he has recovered?'

'I left un readin' football results in *T' South Sussex Star*, Mis' Fairford. But niver a word will un say about who un sweered th' Oath to.'

'How *very* annoying.' And Flora reflected for a moment while Nancy stared placidly out of the window at the twilight.

'I have it!' suddenly said Flora. 'You must ask him to come and see me, Nancy. Then *I* will ask him.'

'I doubts if un wull come, Mis' Fairford.'

'Why not? We are second cousins three times removed.'

'Ay, but tomorrow evenin' us ull be main moithered wi' th' beetroot dryin' for th' winter, Mis' Fairford.'

'Tomorrow evening will be too late, Nancy. Reuben must come tonight.'

'Ter-night! Oh dear-me-soul! Ter-night!'

'Certainly tonight. The Conference ends on Saturday, and I must return to town. I should like to see the Starkadders back at Cold Comfort by Sunday morning.'

'In time fer eleven o'clock church!' said Nancy raptly.

'My own thoughts exactly.' Flora bestowed upon her a glance of approval, suppressing the thought that if eleven o'clock saw the Starkadders filing into church next Sunday morning, the Starkadders would be changed indeed. 'You had better go now, Nancy,' she continued. 'I shall expect Reuben at midnight.'

'Alack, Mis' Fairford! Midnight!'

'Yes, I realize that his beauty sleep will be curtailed, and I am sorry to name so late an hour, but by that time the ladies and gentlemen will all be talking or otherwise engaged and not so likely to disturb us.'

At the door Nancy lingered.

'Please, Mis' Fairford, how wull ee get 'em all whoam from South Afriky so soon?'

'By cable and aeroplane, Nancy. It *is* possible to use such

107

devices for good, and this is one of the occasions when it may be done. Good night.'

The evening drew peacefully on into night. Flora finished her letters, embroidered a small rodent upon a garment for her youngest daughter and read one chapter of an enjoyable stodgy novel. When she shut the book and glanced at the clock, she saw that the hour wanted twenty minutes of midnight. A distant steady roar of conversation pierced by an occasional nervous scream came from the Greate Kitchene, where the delegates were assembled, but fortunately none of them came bothering into the Green Parlour (she could not learn to think of it as the Quiete Retreate), and she was peacefully gazing out through the window, open to the warm dark night, when she saw a light, low down near the ground, moving across the Big Field.

It could not be Reuben's mog's-lanthorn, for Reuben would not come from that direction, but it was a lantern, and whoever bore it was moving in a straying, uncertain manner towards her, pausing every now and again as if to search for something lying on the ground.

The light was now no farther than twenty feet from where she sat.

She leant out of the window and called clearly.

'What are you doing?'

Instantly there was a loud shriek and the light went spinning wildly away and then went out. It is a Starkadder, thought Flora, and sat down to wait.

Pretty soon she heard gasps and faltering footsteps and then a voice, which was familiar though unidentifiable, muttering in the darkness.

'Me an' th' water-voles, we've had it. Niver no more, niver no more,' and the next instant Urk staggered up to the window and his white-and-purple face glared in at her. He wore a frock coat stained with earth and dew, and his top-hat was stove in at one side.

'I am sorry I alarmed you,' remarked Flora pleasantly.

'Arter twenty years! Ten generations o' water-voles has lived an' loved an' whelped an' gone to meet their Maker, but you ain't altered a mite, Robert Poste's child, sin' the day you robbed me o' my Elfine!'

'It is sixteen years, not twenty (though I admit that "twenty" gives a fruitier ring to your sentence). And surely more than *ten* generations of water-voles? (Do come in, won't you? The dew is falling. I am expecting Reuben at any minute for a little talk).'

'What do town-dwellers know o' water-voles, Robert Poste's child?'

'Next to nothing, I am happy to say, and do you think you could manage to call me Mrs Fairford?'

Urk stared at her with a stony, glozen expression.

She passed a light cane chair out of the window to him, saying winningly, 'I do wish you would sit down,' but he flung it from him with an oath.

'As you please, of course. Is something the matter? What are you looking for? Herbs?'

Urk seemed to be recovering his self-possession. He uttered a short, unpleasant laugh and pushed his hat back into shape.

'Nay – no, I should say,' he answered in tones lacking the Starkadder circumlocutions and burr, 'I employ four lads to pick herbs for me, and in any case they would not be working at this hour. The Junior Herb Cullers Union does not allow its members to pick, pluck, procure, or gather any herb, weed, fungus, moss, pulse or bine between ten p.m. and ten a.m. You will be wondering, of course,' holding up a very dirty hand as if to check her question, 'how I contrive to manage the plucking of herbs recommended to be plucked with the dew on them. Your question is perfectly legitimate, and I shall answer it. I employ an extra-union worker, a lad named Hick Dolour. He has been away for a week owing to indisposition, but I expect him back on Monday.'

'How very interesting,' said Flora, relieved to see that he had grown quite calm (as calm, that is to say, as a Starkadder could be) while relating all this. Nevertheless, she hoped that he would go away before Reuben arrived. 'And how is Mrs Starkadder – Meriam?'

But she had said the wrong thing. Urk turned white and purple and bashed his hat in again (at the top this time).

'Curses on her for a grasping she-rat!' he gasped. 'She'll gie me no peace by day or night until her back's covered by a water-vole coat. I ha' offered her coats o' ivery other fur, ay, an' *bought* her one, tu, a main gurt mantle o' Siberian Swamp Rat at a sale in St Leonard's; but 'tes in vain – it's no use, I should say. She du know full well' – he paused and gulped – 'what water-voles du mean ter me, iver sin' I were a liddle ninnet up at our Ticklepenny's Well. So on dark nights she du send me forth to slay 'em.'

'Why on dark nights?' asked Flora, glancing unobtrusively at the clock, which said five minutes to twelve. 'Surely that makes it more difficult to see them?'

'Nay. On dark nights they holds their parliaments.'

'Do they really? I had no idea.'

'Why should ee hev? They keeps theirselves to their-selves, th' water-voles du. But they're gettin' wise an' cunnin', the water-voles are. They're leavin' Sussex an' settlin' theirselves in Hampshire. Niver a vole did I find this night.'

'I am glad to hear it. I cannot say that I am surprised at Meriam, because I remember what she used to be like, and I suppose she is still the same, but it does seem a pity about the water-voles. Have you seen Ticklepenny's Well lately? You always took such an interest in it, I remember.'

'Nay, I niver goes theer. It fair curdles my belly ter see ut. Th' well! wheer I used ter spit down into th' dark secret waters!'

'Yes, it must be very upsetting for you. There is no water there now, you know.'

'*Th' water knows.*

An' th' water flows,' crooned Urk, gazing off through the darkness towards Ticklepenny's Field, 'Ay, it's gone away after th' water-voles, th' water has.'

'It would be a good thing to get the well working again, with constant cold water and a bucket. Don't you agree?'

After a longish pause Urk made the helpful remark that there was now a curse on the well, so that neither water nor water-voles could return to it.

'Surely it is simply a question of removing the bricks which block the hole where the stream enters?' said Flora.

'Nay. Ye dunna know. 'Tes a curse.'

'It's bricks,' muttered Flora, but did not argue the point,

for his interest was aroused and she did not want to annoy him.

She was about to ask him *why* he let Meriam drive him out at midnight to hunt water-voles when there was a bang on the parlour door, and Reuben slouched in. He looked pale and sullen, and when he caught sight of Urk he started back, crying:

'Treason, treason! What's yon goglet o' tractor oil doin' here?'

'Don't be silly, Reuben; Urk was out hunting and he saw the light from the window and just came in for a chat,' said Flora.

'Ay, huntin' on my land.'

'Very poor land it is, too,' retorted Urk, in the oleaginous and superior voice he now used all the time except when he grew excited. 'Nothing but Live-and-Let-Live and Pussy's Dinner growing everywhere, and never a water-vole on the place.'

'An' whose fault? An' whose fault?' Reuben burst out passionately, stepping forward and grasping Urk by his shirtfront and hauling him bodily in through the window. 'Who ran off like a vole wi' his belly full, an' left me here to till an' toil alone? Ye were th' first to go, Urk Starkadder, an' I'll lay ye'll be th' last to come back.'

'Excuse me, Reuben, I was *not* the first to go. Pa was the first to go, as you know well. On the night of the last Counting, before Grandmother left for Paris, Pa went off to catch the milk-train in Agony Beetle's brother's van, and never came back. So why impute to me a priority I cannot justly lay claim to?'

'But ee was the next to go, earwig-shard that ee bee'st!'

112

'Do sit down, please, both of you,' said Flora firmly, shutting the window and indicating two chairs. 'I am glad you have come, Urk, because now we can arrange about re-doing the well; I have always regarded it as your especial interest, and I rely on you to climb down it and remove the bricks when the time is ripe. Now, Reuben, please, if you will just unswear that Oath you took about ploughing the land with the lone hand, we will have the male members of the family back here on Sunday morning in time for eleven o'clock church.'

But Reuben uttered a great cry and sprang from his chair.

'Niver, Cousin Flora, niver in thissy world nor th' next! Unswear me oath! I'd liefer lie cold an' mortsome out on Ticklepenny's under th' liddle sparkly stars, I'd liefer cut th' fursome white throat o' our Hymie th' Angora rabbit, I'd liefer —'

'Yes, I gather what you mean,' said Flora patiently, 'and I quite see that there are difficulties. I thought there would be. But if you don't care to unswear the Oath yourself (I'm not suggesting you should *break* it, you will notice, only that you should unswear it), why not ask the person you swore it to to absolve you from it?'

Reuben flung up his massively-thewed arms with a wild laugh and turned to Urk.

'She dunna understand. It needs Starkadder blood to unnerstand,' he said.

'I have always understood that my mother was a sister of Aunt Ada Doom,' said Flora, with dignity. 'It is true that I have not inherited *some* of the family characteristics, but I certainly understand the nature of an oath. What I cannot understand is your refusal, when you see what a state the farm is in, to unswear it.'

'I must be getting along,' interrupted Urk, importantly, glancing at a platinum watch on his hairy wrist. 'The wife will be expecting me.' He turned to Flora. 'Personally, I see nothing wrong with the farm, except that –'

''Cept that her beant a farm no more an' there beant no Starkadders a-tillin' o' her breast,' interrupted Reuben, gritting his teeth.

'– Except that parts of the land are overrun with weeds of a non-commercial type and – and,' his voice faltered and changed, 'an' th' well wheer th' water-voles an' me used ter chase each other roun' and roun' when we was liddle is all dried up, an' th' waters hev followed me liddle playmates into th' Great Dark.'

'There you are, you see,' put in Flora. 'Reuben loves the land, and you have – er – childhood recollections associated with the well. I do really think, Urk, that *you* ought to persuade him to unswear that Oath.'

'Keep yer oily tongue off of me!' shouted Reuben, towering over his brother. 'Persuade me! Let un try, an' see what un wull git. Un hasna' forgot what I did to un when un tried to persuade th' sukebind rights off of me.'

'The sukebind rights?' said Flora.

'Ay. Th' right to pick un off th' farm lands an' dry un up, an' – an' – use un.'

'I have, among other enterprises, a small commercial establishment in one of the coastal towns, where I am a stockist of herbal specialities,' said Urk rather hastily, 'and I did at one time, on my wife's advice, suggest that the sukebind might be medicinally utilized. My wife, who has psychic powers, practises cheirotherapy under the pseudonym Madame Zulieka, in premises above my own, and it was she who proposed to prescribe it for her clients. But it was only an idea. Nothing came of it.'

'No, but ut would hev, if so be as I hadn't bashed ee,' said Reuben.

'Do let us get back to the point, Reuben,' interrupted Flora. 'I want to know who you swore that Oath to. Do tell me, won't you?'

Reuben looked at his cousin. She was pale from the lateness of the night (for Flora was one who must have her eight hours) and a dark gold curl had fallen over one eye, but she was returning his sombre gaze with a cheerful one of her own. His brown face suddenly rippled with feeling, like peaty waters beneath the wind.

'Ee do wish well ter me an' mine, Cousin Flora,' he said hoarsely.

Flora inclined her head. It was nearly half-past one.

'Ee has allus wished th' farm well, tu.'

Again Flora inclined her head.

'There's no self-seekin' in ee nor yet hasty grabbin, nor yet do ee tear up th' innercent liddle grasses,' flinging a glance at Urk, 'for to make nasty medicines.'

'Of course not,' said Flora.

'That bein' so,' concluded Reuben, with a throaty groan, 'I'll tell ee, Cousin Flora.'

'Thank you, dear Reuben,' said Flora calmly, and prepared herself to listen to a rambling confession.

However, Reuben had first to bow his head upon his clenched hands. Then he looked up at the ceiling. Then

he looked down at the floor and heaved his shoulders up
and down.

After watching his groanings and forehead-slappings,
Flora said:

'Do buck up, Reuben. It is getting extremely late, and
I *am* so sleepy. What would Nancy say if she could see
you going on like this?'

Reuben shuddered, drew a deep breath, and muttered:
''Tes true. I *mun* force th' words past me lips.'

Then he did some more shudders and breathings.

'Reuben! I shall get really annoyed in a minute!'

'Nay, Cousin Flora. I wull speak, but all in good time,
all in good time,' and he went on shuddering.

The grandfather clock struck two.

At last, with a convulsive effort, Reuben brought out
the words:

'Reuben Starkadder! Aye, 'twas to Reuben Starkadder
I sweered th' Oath! I sweers it to meself!' and fell back
in a chair, which almost upset beneath his weight.

'Then there will be less difficulty about unswearing it than
I anticipated,' said Flora briskly. 'No, Reuben, you don't want
to disturb Nancy and the children fetching out Aunt Ada's
copy of *The Milk Producer's Weekly Bulletin and Cowkeeper's
Guide* at this hour. Just unswear it *quietly*, to yourself, please,
while I draft these cables to send to Grootebeeste.'

For some time she wrote briskly upon leaves of her
notebook, while Reuben indulged in a ceremonial which
appeared to involve calculations upon his fingers and much
silent slapping of his forehead. Urk lingered, gnawing his
nails, and alternately darting glances at Reuben and gazing
sullenly at the floor.

'There!' said Flora, as the clock struck half-past two. 'I will send these off first thing to-morrow morning (this morning, that is), as soon as Howling Post Office is open,' and she waved the sheaf of pages at Reuben. 'Please have the buggy ready at ten minutes to eight, Reuben, to drive me down.'

'Hev ee sent a message t' each o' th' lads, Cousin Flora?' asked Reuben wonderingly.

'Yes. It means extra expense, of course, but I thought it the wisest thing to do. A single cry for help addressed, for example, to Micah, would not bring them *all* home.'

'Ee speaks true, Cousin Flora. They be main jealous o' one another, be th' lads.'

'So I seemed to recollect. So I have sent a special appeal to each one, saying that he, and he alone, can save the farm from a fate worse than ploughing under.'

'Gorms, Cousin Flora! What fate could be worse nor that?'

'Each Starkadder will decide that for himself, Reuben, and I feel pretty confident that all tomorrow we shall be receiving cables from the – er – lads, announcing their immediate return. Mud is thicker than water, you know, and remember how muddy Cold Comfort is in the winter.' Then she turned to Urk, and said:

'Will you look in on Saturday morning, Urk, and we will arrange about your climbing down the well to remove the bricks.'

'I shall most certainly do nothing of the kind, Mrs Fairford. To start with, I doubt if the Central Herbalists Federation would permit me to do such a thing.'

'I cannot see why they should object to your popping

down a well to shift a few bricks. It is not as if you were herb-picking out of hours.'

'And it would probably get me into trouble with the Well-Brick Removers Union,' Urk continued, but in a less decided tone.

'You just go ahead and move those bricks, Urk. Then they can argue it out between them. You will probably be a Test Case.'

'I do not wish to be a Test Case, Mrs Fairford.'

'Nonsense. You know you will love it. And now, as we have arranged everything satisfactorily, and as it is nearly three o'clock, I suggest that we all retire. We shall need our strength for tomorrow, which will be a busy day. Good night to you both.'

Reuben and Urk seemed inclined to linger and discuss the night's work (when was a Starkadder ever ready for bed, except in certain circumstances?), but Flora waved them off with her sheaf of cables, and presently had the satisfaction of seeing them tramping across the grey fields in opposite directions. Then, with the intention of brewing for herself some hot milk, she went yawning into the Greate Kitchene.

All was silent in the light of the summer dawn except for someone snoring uncomfortably in a corner whom Flora did not bother to identify. She scalded the milk, and was just carrying the tray along the corridor leading to the attic staircase when a bedroom door opened and out bounced Mr Mybug.

'Hot milk! "Smashing"!' he exclaimed, and was about to help himself from Flora's little jug when Flora wafted it away, saying firmly:

'This is for me, Mr Mybug. There is plenty of milk downstairs if you want some: I understand that Lady Hawk-Monitor sent us down a churnful from Misdemeanour yesterday evening. How, if I may ask, did you know that I had hot milk to spare?'

'Saw you in the Greate Kitchene out of my window. I couldn't sleep,' and Mr Mybug's voice took on a more sombre note as he plomped himself down (greatly to Flora's dismay) upon the bottommost stair of the flight leading to her attic. Mr Mybug then gazed up at Flora, reminding her of a dog she once owned named Nimbo who had always looked in need of help. Mr Mybug wore pyjamas too small for him and a dirty old macintosh.

'This week has been Hell for me,' he began cosily. 'I didn't think it could happen to me. I thought I was safe in a sublimated ethos of my own devising. Well, I'm awake now,' and he gave a brutal realistic laugh.

This was unfortunately true. However, Flora could not very well climb past him, so she drank some hot milk and glanced at one of the many grandfather clocks ticking about the farm nowadays. It said a quarter to four and the birds were singing.

'It's a platitude, of course, that time is measured in terms of our own response to it, but this week I've proved it in "blood, sweat, toil and tears".'

Not toil, thought Flora, drinking some more milk. She did not say anything; she did not even wonder what was coming next, for years and years of listening to people had taught her that if she just kept quiet and sipped or sewed and never looked shocked, there was literally no limit – *no limit at all* – to what people would tell her.

Sometimes, however, she did have to put in a word, in case people should round upon her and savagely accuse her of being a happy pudding, and as this invariably meant the prolonging of the monologue, and as she rather suspected that Mr Mybug would do one of these pounces in a moment, she waited until he had finished a rambling Freudian analysis of Mdlle Avaler's powers of attraction, then slipped in cordially:

'Yes. It must be awful for you.'

But it was too late.

'"Must" be? God, what does a woman like you know about Life?' snarled Mr Mybug. 'What do *you* know of those thwarted ardours that keep the flesh palpitant, the senses astretch? Married to a parson, mother of five children! Pah!'

There really did not seem to be any answer to this, so Flora drank some more milk. The sunlight was now pouring in through the windows.

'The last day!' said Mr Mybug bitterly, and to Flora's relief he got up off the stairs. 'And tomorrow . . . I shall be back in Fitzroy Square.'

'Have they done the ceiling yet?' enquired Flora, beginning to mount. 'I do hope so; nothing is more uncomfortable than workmen in the house.'

'I neither know nor care. Rennett sees to that sort of thing; Rennett interviews the builder; Rennett is the practical, the unadventurous, the prosaic side of me.'

'I am so glad she is well. She must come to tea as soon as I am at home again, and bring Clifford and Alastair and Trafford,' said Flora. 'Good-bye for the present,' and she smilingly shut her bedroom door and turned the key rather noisily, leaving Mr Mybug alone with his sufferings. She then went to sleep for four hours before meeting Reuben at eight o'clock, feeling that she deserved her rest.

She returned to the farm well content on the following morning, having sent off the cables at Howling Post Office, and as she was entering the Greate Laundrie in search of breakfast she was greeted by a voice, at once pert, self-satisfied, and not quite sure of itself:

'Marnin', Mis Fairford. Don't expect ee reckernizes me.'

'How are you, Rennett,' replied Flora, shaking hands with Mrs Mybug and feeling relieved that Mr Mybug would now have to mind his p's and q's. 'How nice to see you again. Have you come down for the Party to-morrow evening?'

'Natcherally. I comes by th' milk train. There's no keepin' me away, Hubby says, when there's junketin's and prancin's afoot. I've brought me ball-gownd, an' all. 'Twas a friend o' Hubby's did design it an' be-wove it tu. It be all over masks of fiends.'

'How original,' said Flora, thinking that nowadays moss-rosebuds would have been far more original and deciding that she could not think Rennett's new style (bun, black sweater, red dirndl) an improvement upon her old one (bun, stuff gown, elastic-sided boots). However, when living in Fitzroy Square one must do as the Fitzrovians did, and in those circles Rennett was doubtless considered a beauty. 'Have you brought the children?' she went on.

Rennett nodded towards three little boys with red cheeks and black curls who were playing near at hand.

'Natcherally. There they be. Hubby do love 'em dearlie,'

she said, with lowered voice and some return of her former timid manner, 'but he would sooner die nor tell.'

'I hope you have breakfasted?' said Flora, preparing to go into the Greate Laundrie for her own breakfast.

'Natcherally. Wi' th' lasses in th' Greate Barne. They begins to show their years, don't ee think?'

'"*Hope long deferred maketh the heart sick*",' quoted Flora, with a note of reproof. 'They have not enjoyed your advantages. But their time of waiting is nearly over. By Sunday morning the Starkadders will be home again.'

'So I hears,' said Rennett. 'And th' lasses is wild wi' joy, trimmin' bonnets an' puttin' frills on petticoats. 'Tes a brave sight, surely.'

Flora was pleased to hear her say so, for it proved that the best qualities in Rennett Starkadder's nature had survived both the arty-smarty veneer imposed upon Mrs I. Mybug and the lachrymose looseness of outlook which was *de rigueur* in the *Crushed Grape*, a public-house in Charlotte Street frequented by Mr Mybug and his friends.

The morning passed comparatively peacefully, though a feeling of expectation, like an insidious perfume, was beginning to pervade the farm. It was diffused both by the delegates, some of whom were looking forward to the Party on the following evening, and by the Starkadder maidens, whose excitement mounted steadily as the day drew on. Wild snatches of song containing references to true hearts, long years, and the humbler types of field vegetation burst occasionally from the Greate Barne or broke the silence in the farm bedrooms. Sheets and blankets were laid out to air on the meadow grass. So were mattresses, pillows, bolster cases and quilts – honeycomb, marcella, and patchwork. It occurred to Flora, seated in the shade of the runner-bean rows and slicing beans for luncheon, that in fact most of the lasses' attention was being paid to future sleeping arrangements at the farm.

Who should approach her, to her extreme dismay, when she had been at work for some twenty minutes, but Mr Claud Hubris, accompanied by a small Operating Executive.

'Good morning,' said the small Operating Executive politely to Flora. 'Have you seen Mdlle Avaler?'

'She has gone for a walk with Mr Jones,' Flora replied.

Mr Hubris turned copper-colour, and the small Operating Executive braced himself to catch him in case he fell. Mr Hubris managed, however, to make a movement of his great hand, and the small Operating Executive, still keeping himself braced, again addressed Flora:

'How long ago?'

'About ten minutes ago. They went,' added Flora, 'towards that wood over there,' pointing. 'The far one,' she added, 'not the one near the road.'

The small Operating Executive now gazed fearfully at Mr Hubris, waiting for the next order. Flora placidly continued to slice beans. Mr Hubris directed a glare like a blow-lamp in action upon the far wood and was silent.

After this had been going on for what seemed a pretty long time, Mr Hubris waved away the small Operating Executive, who made off at the double, and surprised Flora very much by sitting down upon the bench at her side. She would have felt more at ease with an honest-to-god tiger, but she immediately decided to pursue her accustomed course of action when confronted by an unexpected and disagreeable situation – namely, go on in silence with whatever she happened to be doing.

'Want to make some money?' began Mr Hubris, in a voice rusty from brow-beating fellow directors – but slurring the last word even as a cannibal slurs the word 'meat'.

Flora replied cautiously that money was often useful.

'Going to Cornwall this autumn, aren't you?' went on Mr Hubris, without condescending to explain how he came to know this fact. 'What's the place like? Sheltered? Pretty? Decent sands?'

'Ugly and pebbly. The sands are exposed, and near the shore there is a large and voracious quicksand. The cliffs are overgrown with nettles, and such birds as manage to survive there are quite ordinary,' replied Flora untruthfully. She spoke at once and with decision, for she wished to end the converstion. Mr Hubris had only begun it because, whenever he was thwarted in any way, his instinct was to offer someone some money (thereby obtaining power over them if they accepted) or set about making some himself.

He stared suspiciously. He was not quite sure about her.

''Pity,' he said at last. 'Nutritional Necessities Incorporated are permanently alert for development sites. We pay a bonus to any operative recommending one.'

'I could not sincerely recommend Creepworthy Cove. I doubt if anyone could develop it.'

'We should put our team of Amenity Assessors on to it. They would assess it from every angle: soil, water, sounds, light, flora, fauna – everything. Table the advantages. Table the disadvantages. Then plot a scheme.'

'It would have to be a good one.'

'It *would* be a good one,' said Mr Claud Hubris, warming

to his work. 'Why, sitting right here without the assistance of the Amenity Assessors, I can think of a scheme. Concrete the cliff-surfaces. Build a grandstand. Run a line of charas to bring people to see people sink in the quicksands. Thousands in it – if thousands are enough for you.'

'But how would you get the people to sink in the quicksands?' enquired Flora, fascinated.

'Sell 'em tickets. Have a merger with the Euthanasia Society and give it eight and a half per cent of the profits. Or sell the cliff tickets to sadists and the quicksand tickets to masochists. Oh, there'd be no difficulty in selling the *tickets*. 'Question is, would the profits be on a paying scale?'

'I think I see Mdlle Avaler over there,' said Flora, gathering up her bowl of beans, 'and she seems to be coming this way. If you will excuse me, I must take these to the kitchens. I have found our talk most interesting. Good morning.'

Mr Hubris did not reply, for he was glowering at Mdlle Avaler, who now strolled smiling towards him. Mr Jones was not to be seen.

'Claude, you look 'ot,' observed Mdlle Avaler, touching Mr Hubris with the very tip of her cornflower-blue ribbon sash, and Beauty led the Beast away.

After luncheon Flora seated herself in the Green Parlour with a novel by that kind and true-hearted gentleman Henry Kingsley to await the arrival of the replies to her cablegrams. The afternoon was fine, and she would have preferred a walk over Teazeaunt Beacon to visit Elfine, but duty must be done.

From her window she had the Greate Yarde in view, and early in the afternoon some of the Managerial

Revolutionaries drove up in a lorry, laden with alcohol and tobacco to be consumed at the Party, which would officially mark the end of the Conference. It took four of them nearly half an hour to carry these comestibles into the house.

Entertaining, unlike everything else, has become simpler, reflected Flora. An Edwardian hostess was expected to provide attractive premises, delicious food and drink, perfect service, and a handsome, well-dressed, agreeable company. In the Second Dark Ages a hostess could give a party in a damp cellar all over beetles and attended by insolent half-wits, and if only the supply of alcohol and tobacco were unlimited, no one would complain.

''Ere's a wire for Rube Starkadder,' said a voice at the window, interrupting her thoughts. It was Hick Dolour, already mentioned as driver of the converted jeep and extra-union picker of herbs for Urk Starkadder. He handed the envelope to Flora. 'My, my. Wot's cookin' here?' he added, surveying the lorry in the yard and various floral decorations in process of erection in the Greate Laundrie, and he rode off on his bicycle, uttering wolf-whistles.

Flora looked thoughtfully at the telegram. So much depended upon what it said! Should she open the envelope? No, that might enrage Reuben. She gathered up her skirts and went across the fields to his cottage.

'Nay, take un hence, Cousin Flora. 'Tes a message o' fear an' woe; they allus is,' said Reuben fearfully, interrupted while breaking the leaves of the young plants to shade infant cauliflowers.

'Of course it isn't, it's from one of the – er – lads. Do read it!' said Flora.

After some hesitation –

'Whoam, whoam, like a wounded maggit,
Love, Ezra.'

Reuben slowly read aloud, and scratched his head.

'Do ee reckon that means he's a-comin', Cousin Flora?'

'Honestly, I'm dashed if I know, Reuben. What do you think? You know him better than I do.'

'Nay, none knows our Ezra well, me least o' all. 'Tes a waverin', wanderin', wearisomin' soul.'

'Oh well, then that's just the kind of cable he would send, isn't it? I expect it does mean that he is coming. But I am sorry he feels so low as to describe himself as a maggot. He won't be much use on the farm.'

Reuben uttered the short, guttural sound which served the Starkadders as a laugh.

'Nay, Cousin Flora, ee mistakes. "Maggit" du be short fer marsh-tigget, like. Our Ezra means he'll be whoamin' like a marsh-tigget to uns rest.'

'In other words, he *is* coming?'

'Ay – if so be as we reads his meanin' aright.'

He readily agreed that Flora should open any other cables that might arrive during the day, and then she hastened away to tell the good news to Jane, otherwise Our Ezra's Bespoke. Leaving the other female Starkadders burning feathers under Jane's nose and rubbing hartshorn into her hair (she having swooned dead away on hearing the news), Flora returned to the Green Parlour and her book. Excitement among the Starkadder maidens had now mounted to alarming heights, and the run on smelling-salts and whin-water (an allegedly non-alcoholic decoction of hedgerow shoots with a kick like an ack-ack gun) was non-stop.

Shortly before tea was served in the gardens, Hick Dolour appeared at the window again.

''Nother cable for Rube,' he said. ''Ere, what *is* cookin'? Two cables in one day! I carn't come up 'ere again, and that's straight. I gotta class in the Psychology o' the Pedestrian s'evenin'.'

Flora was already reading the message, and only told him in an absent tone that in that case other arrangements must be made.

Don't ee do nothin' till I comes. Micah

said the second cable. This was more satisfactory than Ezra's, hinting as it did at willingness to get to work, and Flora put it in her pocket with a mounting sensation of triumph. She would show it to Reuben after tea.

Hick Dolour, who appeared to have time to spare, was lolling against the window, smoking.

'Course, this aren't in my line, reely,' he began.

Flora was collecting paper table-napkins from a store in the Green Parlour cupboard to furnish out the festal *buffets*, and she replied, still absently:

'So I understand from Mr Urk Starkadder. Do you intend to make herb-picking your profession?'

'Na! 'Erb-pickin' as 'ad it. I'm a stoodent at ther Institoot o' Mechanical Propulsion. (Drivin' Schools, they used to be called.) More scientific than what you might think, mechanical propulsion is. Very interestin'. All these here noo road surfaces needs special techniques to propel the vehicle so as to co-ordinate its functions, see.'

As he uttered the word 'scientific' he lowered his voice, and gave Flora a sidelong beaming glance, as if the very sound of those syllables must fill her with joy.

'Are there many students at the College?' she asked, trying to decide between two designs of paper napkin.

''Bout four 'undred of us. All picked men. It requires a special type er mentality, see. You 'ave to know 'ow the road surface is made, and 'ow the vehicle is made, an' the correct psychological approach to the theory o' mechanical propulsion, see.'

Flora then enquired if he ever heard from his grandfather, Mark Dolour (Reuben having informed her of the relationship between the two).

'Not since last Xmas, I 'aven't. I been waitin' to go in for me Intelligence Test some time, see, 'cause there's a long list. Well, I comes out with ninety-eight per cent! So I drops a line to Grandad about it. Smatterofact I thought he might come across with a bit. Ninety-eight per cent! Why, thass only two points below the Genius ratin', that is!'

'And what did your Grandad say?'

'Why, 'e says if I'm a genius, 'e's Gawd Almighty,' confided Hick in shocked reluctant tones. 'Ignorant. Very be'ind the times, my Grandad is. Well, I must be movin'. Bye-bye.'

Apparently he went to his class, for three later cables were brought up to the farm by Mrs Murther, who had now taken over the duties of post-mistress, and very cross she was at having to toil up Mockuncle Hill three times in one hot afternoon.

The cablegrams said:

> *I allus told ee so I longs to mock at ee in ee's dark hour sincerely Caraway.*
>
> *Curses on ee for a dunderpate Reuben Starkadder see bed is proper aired Harkaway.*
>
> *Arriving ten fifteen by air Ticklepenny's Field Sunday morning willing take on old job same wages plus bonus increased cost of living best respects Mark Dolour.*

'Mark seems slightly changed for the better,' observed Flora to Reuben, as they sat over a late cup of tea in the latter's cottage.

'He allus was a likelyish chap, was Mark. Un'll be main old, though, by now.'

'None of them mention – er – the lasses, Reuben. I do hope that none of them are married again or anything.'

'If so be as any of they du be, Cousin Flora, I knows what I wull do to un,' growled Reuben, swelling.

Flora tactfully changed the subject:

'By air, Mark says. I wonder if they are all coming by air?'

'Ticklepenny's bean't cut for haysel yet. Gurt old aery-plane her wull hev to land in all th' tangle grasses. Hor! hor! hor!'

'That will never do; it will crack itself or something,' said Flora decidedly. 'You must cut Ticklepenny's before Sunday, Reuben.'

'Cut un! Thirty acres of goathling soil our Ticklepenny's

du be, an' me wi'out a reaper nor yet a tractor in th' place!'

'But there are scythes, Reuben. I saw fifteen of them only the other night, arranged over the sink in the Greate Scullerie.'

''Tes man's work, scythin'.'

'Not if it is done in relays. I could help, and Nancy, and perhaps some of the older children, and –' Flora nodded towards the open door, where the Sage, the follower and the helper-out were peacefully partaking of their evening meal.

''Tes a black day for Cold Comfort, when heathens has to scythe Ticklepenny's Field.'

'They are not black, Reuben, they are brown; and besides, what *does* it matter? Now please make arrangements to have Ticklepenny's cut to-morrow night. You had better start late, as the moon does not rise until nine. When it does, it will be full.'

And Flora suppressed a sigh, for she would have preferred scything Ticklepenny's Field by the light of a full moon to attending the Party. However, her plans were maturing successfully, and with the help of that comfort she contrived to pass unruffled through a very disturbed evening. Hacke, Messe and Peccavi suddenly decided that all their works must be instantly packed up in order to leave Sussex on the following morning, as they were due to appear at an Exhibition in Europe in a week's time. Having gobbled their dinner even faster than usual, they all rushed down to the Greate Barne, accompanied by Riska and such of the delegates as had nothing better to do, and began strewing straw, newspaper, rope and packing-cases over the floor and taking pictures down from the walls. Then they began admiring each other's work, and then fell to arguing, and at last, about twelve o'clock, they decided to postpone the packing until the next day, and all four curled up among the litter and went to sleep. Flora, whose services had been fussily requested earlier in the evening, had to step over their recumbent forms to extinguish the lights, which they had of course left burning.

9

The next day was spent by the delegates in bickering among themselves and in coaxing or bullying other people into packing for them, and by Flora in writing a statement of the expenses incurred at the Conference, for perusal by the Treasurers of the International Thinkers' Group and the Weaver's Whim Trust. A cablegram arrived after luncheon saying:

> *For the love o' us all doan't ee doan't ee until I be whoam-gathered yours truly Luke*

followed shortly by another saying:

> *Same as Luke Mark S.,*

and with the arrival of these messages Reuben had now heard from all his relations. Not one had declined (so far as could be deduced from the involved and dramatic style in which they were written) to come home. Indeed, from the speed with which they had replied, Reuben and Flora both deduced that affairs at Grootebeeste were black indeed.

'But we mun niver speak o' it to th' lads, Cousin Flora,'

said Reuben while he and Flora were in the Lytel Scullerie in the late afternoon. Flora was standing upon the massive plate-rack reaching down the fifteen scythes daintily arranged upon the wall and handing them to him as he stood below.

''Tes nigh on three year ago that our Micah did write tu me, answerin' me when I did ask news o' Grootebeeste. *Niver speak o' Grootebeeste,* he did write tu me. So I bewarns ee, coz.'

'Thank you, Reuben. I shall not forget, though I am not in the least likely to want to speak of it, I assure you. There!' and she handed him the last scythe. 'They are not at all rusty; the lasses have kept them bright and clean.'

'Like tu un's true hearts, Cousin Flora. And now th' long, wearisome years o' waitin' is over and un's reward is at hand!'

'Yes. Yes, I hope so,' replied Flora with less warmth; thirteen years of marriage seemed to have softened Reuben's former strictly realistic outlook upon life. 'Let us put the scythes in that wheelbarrow, and then you can take them over to Ticklepenny's and arrange matters with your helpers.'

She anticipated that the Starkadder temperament might prevent Reuben from successfully organizing the cutting of the field, but when she visited the cottage at moonrise that evening, just before the Party began, she found affairs in good train. The scything had begun, and all the cottage party was usefully employed, for even the Sage, whom no one had dared to ask to take a hand, had offered of his own accord to keep watch over a vast Shepherd's Pie baking for the workers' supper. Flora surveyed the scene with satisfaction, and returned to her duties at the Farm. Her eyes were bright and her cheeks glowed beneath her smooth hair dressed with two white peonies, for all went well, and she was content.

The Party went on until seven o'clock the next morning, when the last drop of drink was swallowed and the last cigarette lit, and then there were complaints (as well there might be, only they were not the complaints that a detached observer might have been expected to make in the circumstances). Fairly early in the evening Riska and Peccavi disappeared; that was one good thing; and a little later Mr Mybug went to sleep in the copper; that was another. Peccavi had been in topping form, tripping up the dancers with trick wire flown specially from Lisbon by a friend of his who smuggled drugs, and dropping tobacco ash in the fruit-cup. Mr Mybug said that his malice was deliciously, characteristically unpredictable. Mdlle Avaler looked pure and lovely as an angel in white satin and pearls, and it was shortly after her arrival that Mr Mybug sought sanctuary from Cupid's darts in the copper, emerging at intervals to tell everyone how amusingly cosy it was in there.

Rennett rushed round screaming with laughter and banging everybody except Mr Claud Hubris with a bladder provided by Peccavi. Professors Breed and Brood slowly, smilingly, silently drank, until they slipped down under a *buffet* and gradually became buried in cigarette ash, like contemporary Babes in the Wood. Frau Dichtverworren sat in a corner, watching everybody, and smiling now and again to herself as she made a note.

The massy beams of Cold Comfort Farm's ceilings resounded until they hummed again to the zooming whack of the bladder wielded by Rennett, and to the yells of the scientists, who had formed themselves into a long serpentine procession and wound in and out of the dim rooms screaming: 'We − want − Reality! Give − Us − the − Unsplittable!' Dance bands, relayed from all those foreign stations which sound louder after eleven o'clock, sent forth their cacophany or their briskly indelicate songs into the pandemonium, and the Starkadder maidens, who were supposed to be handing round the food and drink, fled the scene after half an hour of it.

Flora had planned to retire at midnight, but the gaiety developed so rapidly and so soon reached its height that at ten o'clock she found herself compelled to take refuge upon the broad stone mantelpiece of the Greate Kitchene. No one observed her, because she was seated well above the level of the bar and the *buffet*, which were the highest points to which anyone's eyes were raised; and she was even turning the pages of Charlotte Yonge's story *Hopes and Fears*, a copy of which had lain at the back of the mantelpiece for some years undisturbed, and wondering if she could venture to read it by the light of the lamp in its wrought-iron lantern immediately above her head, when, chancing to glance down into the gladsome throng, she met the eyes of Peccavi, enormous, black, glittering with malice. He had returned, and was even riper than usual for mischief.

She could dimly discern Riska in the background, looking like a snake all done up in red sequins and four-inch heels, urging him on. She calmly awaited the instant when he gripped the mantelpiece with both hands, then banged down *Hopes and Fears* as hard as she could upon his fingers, and he fell off into the bowl of steaming punch. This created a diversion, and while Mr Mybug (having struggled out of the copper) was wiping him down, and Messe was ecstatically burning himself with the silver punch-ladle, Flora opened *Hopes and Fears* and began to read.

So great was the confusion below that she knew it would be impossible to make her way through the dancing, drinking, embracing, arguing forms, but she awaited that inevitable moment when they should all surge out to the duckpond and drag off their clothes and jump into it. Then she could slip down and hasten through the deserted rooms and upstairs to bed.

Lifting her eyes occasionally from her book to judge whether that moment was near, she noticed some figures loitering uncertainly, and presently she made out (for the rooms were illuminated only by candles and the farm's home-made electricity) that these laggards were all Managerial Revolutionaries. Flora felt rather sorry for the poor little things, many of whom had specialized in Sexual Psychology or the History of Dancing or the Theory and Practice of Alcoholic Fermentation, but none of whom knew how to kiss or dance or drink. Some of them did try, as the evening went on, but they only made themselves sick. It was a shame, Flora thought.

She half-reclined upon the broad stone shelf, now letting her eyes move along the page of small close print as she followed Miss Yonge's calm but entrancing story, and now lifting them beyond the solid thickness of the old book into the pit beneath, where brilliantly clothed figures (for many of the delegates had essayed fancy dress) writhed and showed off in the dimness, and occasionally a shower of sandwiches, like soundless miniature white aeroplanes, skimmed through the smoky air from the hand of Hacke, who had established himself behind the more distant *buffet* and had set himself the task of filling the punch-bowl with bread. Two powerful wirelesses and the screams of the scientists and the recurrent banging of Rennett's jester-bladder combined with the ceaseless shrill babble of human voices in a din that ended by sending Flora off into a doze.

She was aroused by silence. Lifting her head from *Hopes and Fears*, where drowsiness had pillowed it, she looked down into a dimness pierced by two broad shafts of moonlight. The room was empty. Clocks were striking midnight, and she heard far off the Comus cries and shouts of the rabble. She rapidly climbed down by the projecting iron bars at the side of the mantelpiece where bunched onions had once been hung, and, clasping *Hopes and Fears* to her bosom, sped through rooms lit by flickering candles and failing electric light until she reached the Great Staircasee.

An arm shot out from under a sofa as she trod on the first stair – an arm which, judging by the dripping duckweed yet festooning it, belonged to Peccavi – but a backward kick from her small shoe hurled off his fumbling clasp, and she bounded onwards and gained the safety of her bedroom.

Earlier in the evening the helper-out had informed her that the scything of Ticklepenny's Field was to be followed by A Bit of A Do for the scythers, and now, as she gazed out of her window for a few minutes before getting into bed, she saw a little fire flickering high up on Ticklepenny's ridge and dark figures dancing about it. Strains of music, apparently from an accordion, were wafted upon the gusts of summer wind, which after some doubt she identified as part of a song called *Boiled Beef and Carrots*. They were followed by a wavering Oriental air which threatened to go on for ever, but when it did change (rather abruptly) to a song called *All the Nice Girls Love a Sailor*, she did not hear, because she was asleep.

At this hour, an air liner was leaving the African shores. It was followed by a glider containing an elderly but still handsome bull, reclining upon thick trusses of straw and passing the time alternately by gazing out through the windows dimmed by his own sweet breath and eating the wreath hung round his neck by admirers at the Cape Town airport. Beside him slept Ezra Starkadder, elderly but not still handsome, and in the liner were Micah, Harkaway, Caraway, Luke, Mark, and Mark Dolour, and they were all quarrelling like mad.

10

Punctually at eight o'clock the next morning, refreshed and calm, Flora came down the Great Staircasee.

Stepping over someone lying at the foot, and making a detour round the Laocoon groups huddled all over the Great Kitchene floor, she made her way past the copper in the Great Scullerie, whence protruded Mr Mybug's boots. Festooned all over him like washing was Rennett. At least it is Rennett, thought Flora. There was no sign of Mdlle Avaler, whose national elegance had prevented her from passing what remained of the night upon the floor amidst the ash, drips, wet bread, shoes, braces, duckweed, cigar stumps, cigarette butts, corks, streamers, confetti and other objects.

Flora went into the Great Laundrie, where some of the Starkadder maidens, pale not from late hours but with excitement and hope, were serving breakfast to all the Managerial Revolutionaries, who looked as miserable as their flat, dull little faces would permit.

She sat down immediately opposite somebody hidden by *The New York Times*, who soon lowered it to receive some toast which a Managerial had buttered for him, and revealed himself as Mr Hubris, with the morning light reflected from his pink, massaged chins. Mdlle Avaler was also revealed – for *The New York Times* is a very large newspaper – wearing a delicious travelling costume of fawn linen and gaily eating an egg. Mr Hubris took no notice of Flora, who was glad, but Mdlle Avaler smilingly waved her spoon.

Delegates began to crawl in by twos and threes, most of them dressed ready to leave by car, brake or air, but by far the greater number was still asleep in unconventional nooks. Presently Flora gathered from some remarks shouted by Mrs Ernestine Thump (who had prolonged her visit to include the Party) that Mr Claud Hubris was motoring immediately after breakfast to Gatwick Airport, where his private aeroplane would be at the service of Mdlle Avaler should she require a lift.

Someone at Flora's side started convulsively. She turned, and saw Mr Mybug, who had slouched in unobserved.

'Good morning,' said Flora, and then thought it wiser, judging by his appearance and expression, not to ask him if he had enjoyed the Party.

'How horribly fresh you look!' snarled Mr Mybug.

Being used to this comment upon her appearance from people who habitually sat up until three in the morning, Flora placidly continued her breakfast without replying.

'I suppose I have "had it",' Mr Mybug went on in a dreary undertone. '*I* can't afford diamond bracelets or a trip to the Bahamas.'

'Surely that is all for the best, in the circumstances?' suggested Flora. 'The flesh is sometimes weak.'

'The flesh! That comes well, from you!'

Flora ate some toast and did not reply.

'You simply don't understand, that's all,' said Mr Mybug very bitterly. 'You have ichor in your veins —'

'I beg your pardon?'

'Ichor, not warm red human blood. You've never understood me —'

'It is not my duty to understand you, Mr Mybug. That privilege belongs to Rennett.'

'You've *never* understood me, ever since we first met, sixteen years ago. I told you then that there was a remote, virginal, unawakened quality about you —'

'So you did. I remember now.'

'— and there still is. The truth is — and I only say it because you drive me to it, it isn't a thing a decent human being would choose to say lightly to another — you're both repressed *and* inhibited — and,' concluded Mr Mybug in sorrowful triumph, '*you haven't matured in the least.*'

This awful accusation, which made Flora feel like a bottle of bad Empire wine, ended his tirade, for Rennett bustled in, wearing a hideous tiny hat and accompanied by the little boys, to warn him that he must telephone at once if he intended to secure the car to take them to Beershorn station that evening, and he rushed away. Shortly afterwards Mr Hubris went off, accompanied by Mdlle Avaler and Mrs Ernestine Thump. Both ladies paused to say good-bye to Flora, the young one because good manners were her substitute for a conscience, and the elderly one because she thought that Flora might one day come in useful, like some odd stocks and shares picked up for a song; you never knew; the most unexpected things did.

'Robert Poste's child!'

It was a hoarse whisper through the open window

behind Flora's head, and she turned round and saw Adam Lambsbreath looking in.

'Mus' Urk wants a word wi' ee. He be up at Ticklepenny's Well, all betangled in gurt old ropes.'

'Very well. I will come at once,' and Flora rose and left the table, bowing as she passed them to the Managerial Revolutionaries and Frau Dichtverworren, whom she rightly supposed that she would not see again before their departure.

Her crossing of the Great Yard was brightened by a glimpse of Peccavi and Riska, both clad in holey sweaters, shorts and broken sandals, preparing to set out for Lisbon on a bicycle made for two which Mr Mybug had bought for Peccavi in Haywards Heath, and watched in attentive silence by the three little Mybug boys, whose parents had explained to them what lifelong benefit they would derive from the historic sight. Riska spat at Flora for the last time, and Peccavi put out his tongue as they pedalled uncertainly away. Some of Peccavi's pictures were strapped on the back of the bicycle, and Flora had the satisfaction of seeing them fall off into the road and disappear under the wheels of an unusually large lorry that happened to be passing.

While they were climbing up to the well she heard Adam muttering to himself.

'What is the matter, Adam? Do speak up. What are you doing here, anyway? Surely you have morning duties up at Haute-Couture Hall?'

'I seeks me lost treasure.'

'Oh, your liddle mop. I remember: Ezra was supposed to have thrown it down the well.'

'Ay. An' what business be'es it o' yourn if a man chooses

to come out of a mornin' to breathe th' air? Here I be, an' here I stays until Ticklepenny's sides be wet once more wi' th' spring watters.'

On their arrival at the summit Flora was disconcerted to see a small behind, clothed in nondescript Starkadder garments, reared against the skyline. The remainder of its owner's person was apparently hanging down inside the well.

'Mus' Urk du be gettin' tu work rightaways,' observed Adam with satisfaction.

Flora was spared the difficulty of attracting Urk's attention by his sudden emergence from the depths. His face was pale and his eyes glittered.

''Tes dry as th' Condemn'd Man on a New Year Day down theer,' he observed in the somnambulistic tones which always came upon him when speaking of the well.

'Never mind, we will soon put that to rights!' cried Flora – more heartily than she felt, for, remembering his reluctance on the previous evening, she anticipated at least an hour of coaxing and urging to get him seriously to work.

But her fears were unfounded, or rather, they immediately took another shape; for, uttering that same low, passionful cry with which he had seized Meriam the hired girl on the night of The Counting long ago, Urk began to run at full speed away from the well, dragging after him a rope attached to his waist. While Flora watched in considerable alarm and Adam banged approvingly with his stick, he ran to the rope's full length, then began to run back again. Faster and faster he ran, until he reached the well's edge. Then, even as Flora started forward to prevent him, he leapt in the air, uttered a triumphant shout, and disappeared into the depths. The rope slid rapidly over the side until it pulled up taut with a jerk, and stayed, quivering. All was silent.

'Oh, good gracious, *what* a silly thing to do!' exclaimed Flora, hurrying forward. 'Really, no one but a Starkadder –!'

But Adam, who had hobbled up to the well after her, now paused. With his head cocked on one side he listened. He held up a gnarled finger. Flora, who simply had not dared to peer into those depths, gazed at him in deeper alarm. What fearful sound did he hear?

Suddenly he uttered his wheezing laugh.

''Tes th' pickaxe!' he cried. ''Tes Mus' Urk's pickaxe a-workin' away! Listen, Robert Poste's child!'

Flora, in her turn, listened. Yes, from deep down under the earth came the muffled yet hollow sound of blows, and then, almost before you could have said something nasty in the woodshed, they were followed by frenzied shouts:

'Help! help! I be whelmed by th' waters! I be drownin' in Ticklepenny's Well!'

'Quick, Adam! Oh, hurry, for goodness' sake! We must pull him up by the rope!' cried Flora, and she caught hold of it and exerted all her strength. Below in the earth she heard a washing, rushing, gurgling noise coming ever nearer, and Urk's shouts were now repeated more faintly and at longer intervals. Her strength was barely enough to move the rope.

'Adam! For mercy's *sake*! What *are* you doing? Come and *help* me!'

The old man was peering intently into the well.

'Nay, Robert Poste's child, niver hasten like thataways. *The hand that's shakin' is ill at bakin'.* Th' spring watter will ride our Mus' Urk up to th' light. I mun seek for me lost darlin'. Ha! du I see her?'

Flora continued to haul the rope with every ounce of strength she possessed. Her face was pale and calm and her teeth bit deeply into her lip. Hang the Starkadders! she thought; they were always in some kind of trouble.

Suddenly Adam uttered a piercing cry.

''Tes her! 'Tes my mippet, lost this many a year! Th' watters hev given her back tu me!' and at the same instant he caught with both hands a small grey stick ending in a mass of dirty matted threads which a sudden freshet tossed up from the well.

At the same instant, too, Flora heard shouts behind her, and the rope was suddenly hauled backwards by strong hands. Gasping with relief, she turned, and saw Reuben, Mr Jones, and Sir Richard Hawk-Monitor and his two eldest sons. She laved her own crimson and smarting hands in the icy water which was now spilling over the lip of the well while breathlessly explaining what had happened.

Shortly afterwards Urk was tossed over the edge, accompanied by an anxious-looking water-vole, which waited just long enough to see him restored to his friends before diving back again.

'Be ee amorted, disgrace that ee be'est?' roared Reuben to his brother, while Mr Jones and Sir Richard tried artificial respiration. 'Who gave ee leave to meddle wi' Ticklepenny's Well?'

'Oh, do give him a chance to come round, Reuben,'

said Flora. 'It was my idea really, and you know we arranged it all the night before last.'

'Ay, now I beminds me. We did. But ut has all been done chancy-hasty,' said Reuben in calmer tones. 'Ah, ee be'es alive, be'est ee?' as Urk stirred and groaned.

Mr Jones and Sir Richard went to work with new energy, and soon had the satisfaction of seeing him open his eyes. (Adam, meanwhile, had gone hobbling rapidly off with his restored treasure as soon as he caught sight of Sir Richard, for he was supposed at this hour to be leading Mishap, Mislay, Misdemeanour and Mistrust down to pasture.)

''Tes done!' muttered Urk, gazing at the well with a rapt expression which his rescuers naturally found most annoying. 'Our Ticklepenny's is fresh an' flowin' agen. An' while I were down theer, brother Reuben, what did I see, think ee?'

His hearers were silent. His pleased expression filled them with forebodings. If something at the bottom of a well pleased Urk, then the odds were heavily in favour of its being something that would render that well unfit for drinking by anybody except Urk, and so it proved.

'Water-voles!' he said, nodding his head round at the circle of glum faces. 'A litter o' ten or more, an' th' pell an' th' mell tu' (the pell and the mell are the water-vole sire and dam). 'An' what were th' liddle lovesights doin', think ee?'

No one cared to hazard a guess, and Sir Richard, who had an appointment in Godmere at ten, looked at his watch.

'Gnawin' their ways through to th' water,' said Urk,

in tones thick with delight. 'Ay, th' water-voles know. An' so ut dinnut need more than one blow o' me pick-axe —'

He paused. He gazed all round him. He clapped both hands to his sides.

'Wheer is ut?' he cried. 'Wheer is me pockut pick-axe as I du cull up th' herbs wi'?'

'At the bottom of the well, my good chap, and you're very lucky not to be there with it,' said Sir Richard rather sharply. 'And now if you will forgive me I really must —'

But before he could finish the sentence Urk leapt to his feet and was running full tilt for the well. A cry — of exasperation rather than dismay — went up from the company, but before he could leap in, he stopped short at the brink.

Three brown, sleek heads broke the brimming surface of the water into ripples, and six delicate transparent paws, while the other six trod water, held aloft the pocket pick-axe.

'Bless ee, my beauties!' crooned Urk, leaning over to take it, and Reuben came up behind him and crossly bundled him in.

Flora thought it best to stroll home and put some cream on her smarting hands.

She passed the remainder of the day peacefully enough, for she pleaded that the excitement of the morning had given her a headache which must be nursed in the Green Parlour all the afternoon. Phoebe fluttered in at four o'clock with a tray of tea, looking like a flushed and excited sheep, and Flora partook while glancing through a book of poems called *Thrush-Notes* that Adam had left for her that morning. It was by E. H.-M., and contained the following dedication:

> 'To my Best Friend with the
> Author's grateful admiration
> and tons of love.'

The poems showed a nice nature but were technically weak.

Sounds floated in to her occasionally: sounds softened and made pleasant by distance. Even shouts of 'Be careful! My vork vill broken be! Ach, vot it in Inklandt suffers!' took on a melancholy charm, an almost Venetian cadence, as if Canaletto himself were calling across the flushed evening lagoons, when heard at a distance of four hundred yards; and numerous bumps, thuds and crashes only sounded like an air raid on some other town than one's own. About half-past five Mr Mybug, wearing a colourful lumber-jacket, dashed in to make his farewells.

'God, what an afternoon! We've been moving *Woman with Wind* and *Woman with Child* into the lorry. (You're very *peaceful* in here, I must say, but the backwater is your native element, isn't it?) Well, "bye-bye". Post those figures to the Trust, won't you, and see that Meutre gets the bill for last night's "do".' He wrung her hand. 'See you soon in town. I must fly.'

And he flew, with the colourful lumber-jacket fluttering behind him like the tail of a nightmare peacock. Flora had not taken him into her confidence about the return of the Starkadders, and therefore he did not know that these were the last account sheets the Weavers'

Whim Trust would ever receive from Cold Comfort Farm.

Presently she heard Mr Jones' discontented voice enquiring if anyone had seen Mrs Fairford; he wanted to say good-bye to her. She kept quiet, and at length he gave it up, and the sounds that followed indicated that he was driving off with the Mybugs, Hacke, Messe, *Woman with Wind* and *Woman with Child*.

When the noise of the engines had died off into the stillness, Flora waited another half-hour in case a belated delegate might appear; then she sauntered out into the late afternoon sunlight. Everyone seemed to have gone; a slightly museum-ish peacefulness filled the rooms, and all that remained of the Conference was a leaflet, upon which she could distinguish the words *global importance*, screwed up in a ball in a corner of the Lytel Scullerie. Flora screwed it up still smaller and poked it down a crack in the boards.

She was idly completing this task to her satisfaction when a sound fell upon her ears. Someone in the distance was softly howling. She thought she recognized the voice, and strolled out into the Greate Yarde which, it will be remembered, gave upon the public road.

Yes, there were the Sage, newly girt for departure, and the follower laden with his begging-bowl and crutch, crossing the Yarde just as she came out through the door. The Sage looked at her remotely from beneath the orange folds of his turban, and the follower continued, with tears pouring down his black cheeks, to howl, and beat his breast with one hand, the other being occupied with clutching his master's gear.

'Farewell, Teacher,' called Flora, and they both stood still and regarded her, the follower squinting out of eyes made smaller than ever by grief. 'I fear that you have not acquired merit from the Conference?' she went on, coming up to them.

'How could it be possible to do so, daughter? This meeting was called by Monkey, Monkey was present throughout, and Monkey alone will rejoice in the results.'

'Didn't you even enjoy the change of air?'

'All air is alike to the Enlightened, daughter. Yet it is possible that this one' (touching his breast) 'and that one' (indicating the follower) 'acquired a little, a very little, merit by contemplating the hills and the sky. But none of the feet of those whom I have seen here are set upon the Path.'

'I rather thought you would say that,' said Flora.

The Sage was looking at her with closer attention than he had ever before bestowed upon her, and feeling certain that his next remark would concern her own feet and the impossibility of their ever being set upon the Path while she was so fond of managing things, Flora said rather hastily to the follower:

'You are sad to go away, brother.'

She did not know what else to call him. It must be twenty-five years since anyone in England had called anyone else *my good man*, *mate* he would not have understood, and *comrade*, once the name of affection between rough men-at-arms, now had boring associations.

He began to howl again, with his eyes shut.

'It is all illusion,' said the Sage, looking down at him as he stood there, small and black and drowned in tears. 'Illusion, and the evil of desire. He loveth the one who helpeth with the washing of the pots, he loveth the children of the house, he even loveth me. He desireth to stay here and love them, he desireth to go hence with me and love me. He is all desire. Hence, he is all evil.'

At this the follower howled aloud and pulled out some of his hair.

'Well,' said Flora, seeing that she could be of no practical use here, 'you must go your way and I mine, Teacher. Farewell.'

'Farewell, daughter.'

He made her a salutation, beautiful, in the brief instant that it lasted, as the pose of a dancing Kali. Then he strode away, and the follower scurried after him. When they reached the summit of the road leading on to Mockuncle Hill and thence to open country, the Sage moved swiftly up to the skyline, was silhouetted there for a moment, and then began to disappear from sight down the far side, but the follower turned back when he reached the top, and, incommoded as he was by bowl, crutch and his fast-falling tears yet contrived to make Flora a clumsy salaam. Then he hurried on after his master.

Flora went to the Greate Barne in search of supper.

The odour of hot bread floated out through the open door, and figures in clean print dresses and shiny boots bustled hither and thither, kneading dough, melting sugar, and dredging flour onto pastry-boards, while filling the air with a ceaseless shrill singing.

'Us be gettin' riddy for us'ns men, Miss Poste!' cried Hetty, flitting by with a stack of soggy turnovers, 'time be growin' short, sure-lie!'

'Now wull ee take a bite o' supper wi' us an' ours, Miss

Poste?' asked Jane persuasively, pushing a great green egg all over straw and bits under Flora's nose. 'Us knows ee's heart is well set us-wards an' ours-wards.'

Flora accepted with a smile, and took a seat between Prue and Phoebe at the trestle table where the homespun cloth and the large crackled plates were arranged, but she had hardly raised the first spoonful of the great green egg to her lips when Letty started up with an eldritch cry:

'An airyplane! I hears an airyplane! Maidies all, 'tes our menfolk come whoam!'

Jane snatched up the soggy turnovers, Phoebe caught at a jug of whin-water, Prue and Letty each seized a leaden loaf, while Susan swooped upon the bowl of boiled eggs, and they all rushed to the door. Flora (pausing only to drop the great green egg under the table) hastened after them, out into the Greate Yarde where evening shadows were lightened by the last sunrays shining upon the farm-house roofs. A very large white liner was just crossing through the full sunlight of the upper air immediately overhead, and they all screamed and pointed. In another moment a glider followed it into view, and they all screamed and pointed again. Then seven female forms in long skirts, some wearing large straw hats and some with streaming hair, began to hurry up the slopes of grass rising towards Ticklepenny's Field, shrieking and brandishing loaves, jugs and tarts, and stumbling as they ran. Flora followed at a more restrained pace, rather vexed that the Starkadders had returned some seventeen hours earlier than they were expected. But wasn't it just like them?

As the maidens (it has been convenient throughout to call them so, though in fact some were married) reached

ummit of the slope, the liner was just making a rather
erior landing in Ticklepenny's, and Reuben and his
family could be seen running over the field towards it. It
looked larger and whiter and more disturbing than ever
now that it was on the ground, and Flora felt certain that
if the Sage could have seen it he would have credited it
without hesitation to the account of Monkey.

The glider, meanwhile, had landed upon a haystack.

Reuben's family were now crowding round the liner,
and more sightseers, including Hick Dolour and Mrs
Murther and other Howling villagers, were arriving every
moment, and hurrying up to the white monster standing
amidst the bleached grass.

Suddenly a door in its side opened. A figure stood there,
looking bronzed, bearded and very cross. A cheer went up:

'Micah! 'Tes Micah Starkadder!' and Susan screamed
piercingly and swooned. Phoebe dashed some whin-water
over her.

Micah flung up his hand. At once the crowd became
silent.

'My curse be on ye all!' roared Micah. 'Broken reeds
and weak sisters that ye be! Th' stranger's foot be set on
Cold Comfort's hearth an' th' sukebind grows wheer th'
wheat should be settin'! Is this how ye keeps your Oath,
Reuben Starkadder?' pointing at his nephew.

'I niver sweers that sort of a oath, Uncle Micah. Ee
mistakes. What I swears was –'

'Nay, niver answer me! I sees th' answer writ plain fer
all to read. Ay,' and his voice swelled like thunder rolling
round the Draakensberg Ranges, ''twas full time, full time,
Starkadders all, as I did come whoam agen!'

Micah paused, and let his eye slowly pass over the faces of the assembly, which, however, was not so awed by this as he had hoped, because half of it was now interestedly watching Ezra's efforts to coax Big Business out of the glider and down the side of the haystack, Big Business the while looking majestically at Ezra as if to ask him was he crazy?

Micah drew a deep breath.

'Now hear me, all on ye!' he thundered, holding up a very large hand with a brass ring on it. 'Afore ye all I swears a solemn oath –'

'Oh please, *need* we have any more solemn oaths?' It was Flora, who had made her way through the crowd, and now stood at Micah's side. 'They *are* such a nuisance, and it *is* such a bore getting them unsworn again. Do let's get the others out, the maidens are simply longing to see them' (and indeed, other bronzed, bearded faces could be seen peering gloomily over Micah's shoulder), 'and then you can swear it after supper – if you still *really* feel you *must.*'

There was a pause, during which Micah frowned steadily upon Flora. Then:

'I mind ye, it beseems me,' he said at last. 'Ay, now I mind ye well. Ye be Robert Poste's child, and 'twas ee who did presumpt tu set us all by th' ears nigh on siventeen years agone.'

'You can put it that way if you like, Fig Starkadder's child. But never mind all that now; *do* let the others out.'

Here the others settled matters by hurling Micah aside and rushing down the liner's steps. At the same moment Big Business, with an indignant bellow, fell out of the on to the heap of straw which the prudent Ezra been diligently preparing for this very event.

Sobbing with joy, the maidens ran to their men and made to fling themselves into their arms. But not all were received with kindness. Flora heard Ezra accuse Jane of betraying him with the postman, and Harkaway telling Hetty that her letters had been main drearsome and dull, while Caraway contented himself with felling Letty to the earth. Luke and Mark affected not to recognize Prue and Phoebe and roared with laughter at their dismay, but none of the maidens expressed resentment; their meek faces shone with fulfilment as they gazed adoringly, through falling tears, at their men; and when at last a procession set out for the Farm, headed by Micah and Reuben, each Starkadder had beside him a maiden, staggering beneath the weight of his luggage and meekly sucking an exotically flavoured South African lollipop.

'Come, Mis' Fairford!' exclaimed Nancy, hurrying up to Flora with smiling face and a child on either hand. 'Supper be spread below, an' we mun drink ee's health in bracket. For 'tes all along o' ee that th' lads be whoam agen!'

'That is very kind of you, Nancy, but I am going home myself now –'

'Whoam? Ter-night?'

'Yes. I think I see a friend over there who will drive me back to London –' and Flora nodded towards the road a quarter of a mile or so away, where for the last ten minutes a very large open pale blue racing car had been drawn up, containing a small female form dressed in white – 'and my family will be expecting me, you know.'

'I were main set fer ee to sit in church ter-morrer wi' us an' ours, Mis' Fairford.'

'I know you were, Nancy, and it would have been very gratifying to me to come, but —'

Flora paused. Sounds from the farmhouse were coming up through the still, clear evening air. They are best described as roars of surprised fury, and they were followed by the unmistakable sound of Welsh dressers and framed samplers being hurled out of windows.

'Dear-me-love!' exclaimed Nancy.

Flora nodded. 'Reuben must write and explain matters to the Trust,' she said. 'He might suggest that the Starkadders buy the farm back again; they must have plenty of money, for you cannot hire an air liner and a glider for a song, you know. Perhaps they have struck a diamond-pipe on Grootebee —'

'Nay, niver mention Grootebeeste!'

'All right, then, I won't. Now, Nancy, I must really be going' (for the small female form in the large pale blue open car had begun beckoning). 'My case is packed and ready in my room. Could Charley bring it up to me?'

Away ran Charley, eager to get a closer view of the bonfire now blazing in the Greate Yarde, and after Flora and Nancy had exchanged a cordial farewell, Nancy went down the hill with the children, and Flora walked over to the car.

'Hullo, darling,' said Mrs Smiling. 'What in heck is going on down there? Did you have a nice time? Has the weather been good? In London it's been snowing.'

'The weather has been warm, and we've had thick dews

and early morning mists and pigeons calling all day in the woods.'

'Aren't you clever. All your children are well; I saw the spiv in the Park this morning with Emilia, and he told me so, with his dishonest face wreathed in smiles. Flawra, what *is* going on down there? Here, have the glasses.'

She handed them to Flora, who adjusted them to her own sight, and looked.

Caraway's face, contorted with passion of some kind, swam into her field of vision as he rushed across the Greate Yarde pursuing somebody with a chopper, and when she moved the glass a little to the left she focused on Mark Dolour, slowly breaking up some article of furniture to feed the bonfire and at intervals striking matches along the snowy walls. The clangour of wrought-iron signs being kicked across a stone floor came from the Greate Scullerie, and her last sight of the farm was a glimpse of Ezra, stooping in one of the numerous little gardens to score the superb turf with an old knife. Beside him lay a mound of young cabbage plants.

As she returned the glasses to Mrs Smiling, she saw Adam Lambsbreath hobbling down over the ridge at the far end of Ticklepenny's Field, looking exactly the same as he had for the past fifty years, and followed by Mishap, Mislay, Misdemeanour and Mischance. He saw Flora, scowled, and gazed away from her. He was evidently leading the cows down to the farm on a visit, for, when they saw Big Business still sulking by the haystack where his outrageous descent had occurred, they all lifted their heads and mooed in shy, dutiful welcome.

Charley now came panting up with Flora's case.

''Tes turrible down theer, Mis' Fairford!' cried Charley, his eyes bright with entertainment. 'Our Micah du be a-cursin' of Feyther, an' Feyther du be a-cursin' of un back agen. Our Mark an' our Luke du be fightin' in the Greate Barne, an' th' maidens be weepen all. There be cakes for all, an' pots o' bracket an' whin-water an' they sugar things fro' South Afriky. Ay, an' our Caraway he du be pushin' all t' furniture out of window! 'Tes wunnerful turrible tu see, Mis' Fairford. Wull ee come down an' see ut, Mis' Fairford, wull ee?'

'No, thank you, Charley. I must go home. Good-bye. If I were you I should get under the table —'

'Oah, I dunna like it theer, Mis' Fairford. I likes fine to see 'em all a-bashin' an' a-cursin'! I mun go now, Mis' Fairford, for fear o' missin' summut!'

He rushed away down the hill, and Flora turned to Mrs Smiling.

'We will go too, Mary, if you are ready? Cold Comfort Farm seems to be itself again.'

www.vintage-classics.info